THE FIFTH ESTATE

In the introduction to the English translation of his first novel, Camon explains that it was to be a 'justification not of his own life but of all my peasant people, the fifth estate, which itself has never told its story, one of enormous heroism and age-old resignation'. The novel attracted eminent admirers: Pier Paolo Pasolini wanted to write the preface to the Italian edition, Jean-Paul Sartre immediately had it translated into French. Both recognized the novel as a faithful testimony to the lives of ordinary people.

Camon calls his novel the 'geography' of the Italian people. It deals with a segment of the population whose customs have remained the same for centuries, unaffected by the cultural and social changes that have revolutionized the rest of Europe. The people do not speak the language of their homeland, but in dialect; they remain transfixed by age-old beliefs, the cult of the dead, departed spirits, fetishism, a 'pagan' Catholicism. They have no wish for involvement in the rest of the world, seeking to remain under an oblivious cloud. Ferdinando Camon chronicles the passing in our own time of an ageless civilization, into which he himself was born.

The Fifth Estate is the first part of Ferdinando Camon's trilogy of autobiographical novels, *Ciclo degli ultimi*. With it he laid the groundwork for a reputation that has now become worldwide. The trilogy has already appeared in translation in the USA, the former Soviet Union, Germany, France, the Netherlands, Spain, Greece, Hungary, Poland, Romania and Argentina.

D1396188

FERDINANDO CAMON

Ferdinando Camon was born in 1935, into a family of peasants living and working in S. Salvaro d'Urbana, near Padua. Journalist, novelist and essayist, Camon is considered by Italian critics to be an 'author of crisis'. He is mainly concerned with the price paid for 'progress' and the extinction of peasant society: 'the biggest world event after the birth of Christ'. His works have appeared in translation worldwide. The author is married with two children and lives in Padua.

FERDINANDO CAMON

THE FIFTH ESTATE

With an Introduction by
the AUTHOR
Translated from the Italian by
JOHN SHEPLEY

QUARTET ENCOUNTERS

Quartet Books

Published in Great Britain by Quartet Books Limited 1994
A member of the Namara Group
27 Goodge Street
London W1P 1FD

Originally published under the title *Il Quinto Stato*
Copyright © 1970 by Aldo Garzanti Editore, Milan
Translation copyright © 1987 by John Shepley

ISBN 0 7043 0202 0
A catalogue record for this book is available
from the British Library

Reproduced, printed and bound in Finland by Werner Söderström Oy

And he knew it, and said, It is my son's coat; an evil beast hath devoured him; Joseph is without doubt rent in pieces. ... And all his sons and all his daughters rose up to comfort him; but he refused to be comforted.

Genesis 37:33-35

CONTENTS

Introduction

This is my first novel, and I wrote it quickly, in a few
months, working on it nights and Sundays. Every
Sunday at dawn, rain or shine, my wife would go out of
the house—a small apartment in a small city at the gates
of Venice—taking with her our two very young children,
so that from eight a.m. until noon I would be able to
make headway on the book. It was to be the justification
not of my own life but of all my peasant people, the fifth
estate, which itself had never told its story, one of
enormous heroism and age-old resignation. Italian cul-
ture at the time was concentrated entirely on the world
of the workers, the city and the factory: Calvino wrote
for the intellectuals; Sciascia pursued the vicissitudes of
the Mafia, and the Mafia became for him a formula
capable of explaining the whole world, which appeared
to him as a struggle between rival clans; Moravia
observed the idle and debauched Roman bourgeoisie, a
human type to whom sex is everything and occupies
head and heart. No one took any interest in the peasant
world, this very vast segment of Italy and Europe. In
order to write this novel I had to imagine a few ideal
readers: Pier Paolo Pasolini in Italy, Jean-Paul Sartre in
France. I must say that both of them proved to be highly
sensitive: Pasolini wanted to write the preface to the

Italian edition, and Sartre had the book translated immediately into French. Then there was a Soviet intellectual named Breitburd, who often came to Italy for congresses and discussions and was astonished that Italian literature never spoke of the peasants. He personally translated *The Fifth Estate* into Russian. He also wanted to translate the next book, *Life Everlasting*, and for this purpose moved into a dacha outside Moscow, but he died of a heart attack halfway through the work, which was then completed by others. "When I took a train across the broadest Italian plain," Breitburd wrote me, "from the most beautiful city, Venice, to the richest one, Milan, I kept wondering what lay beyond the rivers and levees I saw from the window." What indeed lay there?

It was the "fifth estate." A humanity fettered for centuries, untouched by the profound changes that have revolutionized the rest of Europe. A "Third World" oasis, immobile and backward, in the heart of one of the European nations undergoing the most dizzying transformations. A segment of the population that did not even know the language of its own nation, whether spoken or written. Mired in centuries-old beliefs: the cult of the dead, departed spirits, fetishism, the presence of devils, a Catholicism that flowed into paganism, a host of taboos, the absence of a written tradition, the substitution of legends for history. A people from whom everyone fled, intellectuals first of all. Sunk in oblivion, this people had only one wish: to vanish, to be extinguished, without anyone's knowledge.

Having been born in its midst, I was soaked through with its grandiose and wretched, heroic and humiliating myths, like a sponge in a pail of water. These myths, cruel and of the gentlest, hurt me like a tumor: I had to detach them from myself and store them up. This was how the novel *The Fifth Estate* was born.

It is thus a testimony from within. I am well aware that the reader—the European reader, but especially the American one—will find every line incredible, but everything that is told here is strictly true. A people that did not want to be known here finds itself revealed to the reader (the enemy) by one of its sons: in a word, betrayed. From that point on, writing has always been marked for me by these two characteristics: it is a work of liberation, it is a work of betrayal. I did not betray a man, because I did not tell of an individual hero; I told of a community, I constructed a choral novel, whose protagonist is a multitude: my people. The betrayal perpetrated by my writing was thus directed against my roots, against myself. I believe that therein lies the neurotic core of my writing: I write for others, and against myself.

In my own mind, I call *The Fifth Estate* the "geography" of the peasant people. The next novel, *Life Everlasting*, I call the "history." The first tries to tell the story of an archaic community and "the way it works" through a myriad of figures—persons, angels, devils, animals—and a mist of legends; the second isolates, within this galaxy, the bright star of the Peasant Resistance: a barbaric and visceral struggle with neither ideology nor program. The peasant people on that occasion endured massacres and reprisals that no one will ever recount, because history keeps its eyes elsewhere. In *Life Everlasting* I tried as best I could to tell a portion of this saga. In it there is a negative hero, of bestial ferocity. I left him the name he had in reality. He was a colonel in the S.S., a certain Lembke. I did not know that Lembke was still alive. The book, after a series of translations—French, Russian, Hungarian, Bulgarian, Rumanian—was finally published in German as well, first in the Democratic Republic, then in the Federal. There it became a best seller, with this singular fate: Lembke was discovered, and preparations were made to bring him to trial. On the eve of the trial, he died of a heart attack. Since then I find myself thinking of *Life Everlasting* as a rifle shot, fired from Italy at Germany, to strike the heart of an enemy of my people. Thus between vengeance, betrayal, liberation, and condemnation, writing strenuously consumes me, trapping me in a vicious circle from which I see no escape.

Ferdinando Camon

PART ONE

1. The human or almost human figure

My village is a big one but the houses are few and far
between and people don't know each other and the
fishermen who live to the south where the river over-
flows its banks and floods the fields to form a sea ahead
of time, nobody even knew they existed because they'd
never come out in the sun and I was the one to discover
them in one of my rambles off the beaten track, usually
I'd head north passing first of all by the Tojon farm with
its low wide square house with a pointed roof and a
bunch of chimneys set in a funny way in groups some
high some low like tired sentries and it looks like there's
no way any of them could correspond to a fireplace or
stove or maybe they used to correspond when the count
and his family lived in the house but now the count and
his family have moved to Monte Salice and they have a
villa halfway up a hill just about where that low wall
starts which borders the road going up and connects the
little altars marking the stages of the procession of the
Via Crucis and seen from a distance so yellowish and
crumbling in the middle of the vegetation it looks like a
zipper in a piece of green cloth if you look at it with an
uncluttered mind but maybe it's never made that impression on the Tojons because every time they go to the
count to take him the rent money or the first fruits of the
season or the specially raised capons or the kid fattened

up for Easter they arrive with their hearts in their mouths stop in front of the gate and each tries to get someone else to take the responsibility for ringing the bell and when one of the Tojons finally decides they all take off their caps and line up in single file it being understood that it's the one at the head of the line who must carry the tribute and they wait for someone to come and sooner or later a servant shows up who has nothing to do from morning to night and is therefore spoiled rotten and full of his own importance, he opens the gate without saying a word and this already throws the ideas of the Tojon first in line into confusion since having prepared his words he must now discard them because they're no good any more and find other ones anyway they go in and are led into the courtyard passing the servants' quarters and stables and hunting dogs and carefully tended gardens and private chapel where they make a bow and then the servant leads them into a small room whose wooden floor is left unwaxed because these beasts of peasants dirty everything and while they stand there waiting with their caps in their hands and their money in the purse looking at each other from time to time the manager comes in and sits down saying hurriedly all right, let's go, they've never looked the owner in the face and don't know if he's satisfied with them more or less or wants to rent the fields to someone else, once around noon they heard a servant woman in the courtyard ask a little girl who might have been one of the count's daughters signorina what are you having for lunch and the little countess said pigeon livers and even if they live to be a thousand years old they'll always have the desire to eat pigeon livers, so you can just imagine whether the Tojons when they go to their lord and master in such a frame of mind, which anyway is understandable because if the owner takes the fields away from them they're immediately destitute, have any time or inclination to be conscious of that zipper in the green cloth. After the Tojon farm the road crosses the culverts several times and therefore that stretch is called the Crossings, at the largest crossing there's a chapel with the Madonna and in front of it two heavy candlesticks with lead bases otherwise the wind would knock them over, the candles are lit when it's the feast of the Madonna when it's the feast of our patron saint when somebody is sick and when the anniversary of the votive offering for the cholera comes around. At the level of the fourth crossing live the Cojans famous all over the village because they have a crazy daughter with a drooping and drooling lower lip who every so often pulls up her skirts with a sad smile and mutters to her pudenda and famous also for having the finest sow in the village who when she'd give birth used to become rabid and bite anyone who came near her, so that one night old Cojan to get away from her had to leap up and grab hold of the rafters and there he hung with his legs doubled up until morning when his sons freed him by driving off the sow with a whip and pitchfork, this sow as she got old became constipated and so as not to send for the veterinarian who costs a lot of money and to get to his house you have to ride ten kilometers on a bicycle

Cojan decided to do it all by himself and figuring that the animal's intestines were contracted with his sons' help he tried to expand them by sticking a red-hot iron up the sow's behind and in short made her burst with pain squealing horribly all the time. These Cojans aren't civilized people because from time immemorial they've been living in the middle of the Desert, the most godforsaken part of the countryside, where there are no roads and the dark red soil is hard solid difficult to plow because the furrow turns out to be nothing but a sharp cut, it's unproductive and therefore full of wild grapes weeds and thick underbrush hiding the flight of the woodcock or the cautious steps of hares, here the Cojan boys learned to walk on the dry grass in the ditches without making a sound so as to catch stray cats and castrate them in a bloody operation to cut off dogs' tails with one swipe so that they can then heal by themselves to boil hornets in their nests to set fire to grasshoppers in flight to trap a woodpecker that's got inside the trunk of a tree to find the nests of blackbirds so as to drink the eggs to catch snakes by the neck with two fingers so they can't bite, here the Cojan boys would never see a living soul except when the hunting season starts and with the first mists of September the thrushes come down from the mountains in search of the last bitter grapes and the grouse on the ridge raises its multicolored crest and gazes with glassy motionless eyes and flocks of peahens come down veering this way and that and in the shifting fog spot the glimmer of dew on the stubble and the rolling echoes of the first shots warn the

6

hare crouched in the low bushes that it had better find a new shelter every hour sleeping between two roots or under a clod of turf or in a cultivated spot where the plants at dawn give off an odor that confounds the noses of the dogs, then for the Cojan boys the great season would begin when it seemed as though almost every week they'd see the human figure at least from a distance and they knew the places where you might run into hunters namely the high ridges that overlook two stretches of land or the long culverts through which you have to pass or the tree trunks laid across water-filled ditches or the path free of dry leaves that runs through the underbrush, and then the hunter who had fired at a goshawk rising up out of the woods with its slanting flight would follow it with his gaze while it flapped its wings laboriously in the wind and seeing it from afar turn upside down and plummet as though shattered would go to look for it and find it right there at the feet of one of the Cojan boys. For some time now the Cojans have been living in the area of the crossing which is practically where the main arteries of the village meet and here thank God the human or almost human figure can be seen with a certain frequency, but their age-old isolation has chilled the blood in the veins of the Cojans and the Cojan kids are always at the windows with their noses pressed against the glass looking to see who might be going by on the road and if by chance they hear that someone coming on a bicycle is about to stop they rush outside to get a look at him. After the Cojans the road turns and you don't see any houses but they must be somewhere there in the middle of the fields because these lands belong to the Bonomo family who have so many hired hands and these hands must live somewhere or other, anyway the Solimanis also live right there in the middle of the fields they're of Turkish origin as you can tell by their name I've never seen their house but I know where it is more or less because every evening at sunset their peacock lets out two or three squawks that can be heard all over the place, and still farther on is the section with the worst reputation full of thieves shrewd but downtrodden folk who wait till September and then go with baskets and take the plump shiny grapes from other people's fields but always in neighboring villages because in ours it's quite dangerous to steal in fact when the peasants here are afraid they're getting robbed they set up mantraps by sticking willow or plane-tree poles in the ground which they bend back as far as they can and hold in this position by tying them with wire so that if at night someone bumps into the wire the pole is immediately released and packs such a wallop that Onfo for example was found next morning lying on the ground and still unable to breathe properly and they had to take him to the hospital in a gig, and what's more in our village where people have such a strong sense of property there's a night watchman who makes the rounds of the fields to look after things, this watchman has only his right arm and nobody knows how he lost his left one because all we know about his past is that he got out of prison not long ago after serving many years for murder having as a young man killed his girl who wanted to marry someone else, and he killed her by shooting her in the back point-blank with his shotgun making a hole in her this big and at this point whoever is telling you the story shows you with his hands the size of the hole, anyway now they don't let the watchman carry a gun any more his name is One-Arm he makes his rounds armed with a stick with a sharp iron tip and now and then he drops in on families along the way to collect his pay which might be a flask of wine or a dish of polenta or a salami. Still farther on there's the house of Bepi the Friar who as a young man was in a monastery and for years now he's always drunk and with the whites of his eyes glaring bloodshot with malevolent red veins he wears clodhoppers with wooden soles and no laces and no socks he's not strong as a matter of fact when he breathes and especially when he coughs you can hear his breath issuing from his phlegm-choked insides as though through a caved-in tunnel but he's still vicious in a subtle way capable of punishing his little kids with methods that can give you a headache just thinking about it and in fact his three children are growing up wild and scared they never stand still and wherever they are they're always moving two steps forward and two back like hunted animals ready to take flight. In Bepi the Friar's fields is the cemetery where the village of San Marco begins and the cemetery consists of a quarter of a field that for the time being isn't cultivated but is left there for graves, and the graves are marked by little mounds of upturned earth on which flowers are

9

planted for the dead, the cemetery isn't fenced and so it's as though the dead weren't confined to a particular place and in fact you can feel their heavy troublesome presence just about everywhere like the story my father used to tell when we were sitting around the fireplace about one of our ancestors who going by the cemetery one night heard someone weeping and lamenting but when he looked he couldn't see anyone even though there was a full moon and since the sound of weeping had now come so close to him that it was only a step away out of fear he made the sign of the cross and said soul from Purgatory tell me who you are so I can have a mass said for you but by now it was too late the sound was right on top of him or rather it was as though it had poured itself into his ears whereupon our ancestor threw off his cloak and ran away jumping over ditches and hedges and bursting into the house bolted the door behind him and right away he heard something crash against it surely it must have been a soul from either Purgatory or Hell but anyway roasted in the fire because next morning on opening the door he found the scorched imprint of two crossed bones, there's no question but that there are wide openings leading from the other world into this one and through these openings pass not only the souls of the dead like for example the ones that when I'd sit in front of the fireplace on winter evenings and get scared thinking about them would have fun slapping my cheeks so hard that the food popped out of my mouth and I'd pick it up again as quietly as I could without complaining to anybody

10

because the dead are touchy and have all kinds of power over the living, the devil sometimes passes through those invisible openings too, for instance when that ancestor of the Biscazzos was dying and if you want to know what sort of people they were just remember that bis means twice* the priest had gone to hear his confession along with the altar boy and bell ringer who were carrying the holy oil and had sat down beside the straw mattress into which the dying man had sunk so that all you could see was the end of his nose and his little eyes staring motionless at the ceiling and the priest putting on his stole spoke to him softly tell me my son tell me my son what have you done in this life but the dying man kept silent as though he didn't hear with his eyes motionless and so the priest blessed him with the holy water and all of a sudden something like a furious flutter of huge wings was heard in the room and the dying man started to sweat drenching the mattress and with his eyes still fixed on the ceiling kept repeating send that ugly beast away and then the priest understood the ugly beast was the devil in person perched on the rafters and waiting for the man's soul and without looking up in that direction he bowed his head and left the room in defeat.

When I was a child I was always having fevers and nightmares and I'd wake up in the morning with a bitter taste of blood in my mouth and one day my father went out without saying a word and came back in a rage

*I.e., twice stupid (Tr.).

dragging a gypsy woman who had passed along our road a few weeks before and had touched our gate with her hands and looking at me had made the sign of the cross, now my father stuck his fist under her nose and ordered her God damn it that's enough make him get well but she held out until my father knocked her down and put her head on the chopping block yelling I'll kill you and he held her by the hair with one hand and with the other raised the ax and then she said turn the chain on the fireplace and my father turned the chain around and next day I felt better, I remember too that when the Mabile woman wanted to know if her son was still alive she took the missal and opening it to the page for that day made a hole and through the hole she drew a string tied to the key to the door of the house and so the key lay on the words that la Mabile was reading between two candles and since her son was alive the key moved but in little fits and starts as though hobbling on crutches and in fact two years later her son appeared at the bend in the road proceeding with first a step then a hop having substituted a cane for the leg that had been shattered by shrapnel.

Once we get to the San Marco cemetery so as not to leave our village we have to turn left on a path of beaten earth that cuts across land I don't know and which is always under water so that you have to carry your bicycle on your shoulder, this path leads to the Swamp where there's the sinkhole and the water stagnates in little foul-smelling bogs of slime full of earthworms rotting fish and the carcasses of dogs and cows, this is the most isolated place in the whole Po Valley because there are no paths except for the river banks which however are impractical and never lead to any villages but pass in a roundabout way along the far outskirts running every so often into some farmhouse lost in the fog where the inhabitants themselves don't even know what municipality they belong to and anyway they never have any need of documents, with every two or three villages it passes through the river changes its name since the inhabitants communicate little among themselves or not at all and so there's still no uniformity, in our village the river is called Fratta and old Rapacina used to say that it was called Fratta because it was dug by friars and that one of his ancestors recalled having seen as a child the friars digging the river with their shovels. From the low wall of the sinkhole you can see in the distance above the vegetation the red walls of the Bevilacqua castle which is built as an exact square with square towers at each of its four corners surrounded at the top by slender battlements without any ornament or coat of arms and with its uniformly red walls pierced by just a few tiny windows like spyholes, inside the white friars live by prayer and fasting and every Friday flog each other for expiation, the woods in the Swamp echo the sounds of the flogging, and when a woman passes under the walls they cover their faces with their hands and the minute she's gone they rush out egging each other on with pails of water and sponges to erase her disturbing footprints in the dust. Here along the river also live the hog butchers five or six men who don't

13

belong to the same family but every winter form a sort of team, one for example collects the knives another the ax another the tub another the rope another the cart and they make a list of their hog-killing jobs and putting on high boots set out on their rounds scrupulously taking each one in its proper order since this is a rather complicated and responsible business the hog owners in fact have to boil about a quintal of water at a very high temperature and since the indoor fireplace isn't wide enough they light a big bonfire outside besides that they have to prepare a kind of gallows from which the slaughtered animal will be hung by the tendons of its hind feet, when everything is ready the hog butchers arrive pushing their cart they set up the tub which looks sort of like a feeding trough but without feet and wide at the top and narrow at the bottom they set it upside down in the middle of the yard and then one of them goes into the pigsty and sticks a piece of rope in the hog's mouth the hog immediately bites it and holds fast with its teeth then the man passes the ends of the rope around its snout and pulls them tight and so the hog finds itself tied by its nose and can be dragged outside without the rope slipping because a piece of it is held between its teeth it takes four of the butchers pulling with all their might since the hog understands that the situation is serious and digs in with all four feet and so the five of them go forward four pulling and one holding back and squealing with all its might through its locked gums, the hog has a horrible and high-pitched squeal and the children look on spellbound holding their ears, in the end the hog is dragged all the way to the overturned tub where they hoist it up still squealing so that it straddles it with two legs on one side two legs on the other the tail at one end and the head forward and the woman of the house immediately runs to put under the animal's neck the pot in which the polenta is usually made and from which the animal has eaten three times a day all its life and meanwhile the fifth man who up to now has just stood there waiting goes into action with his left hand he feels the hog's neck searching for the proper vein and with a single motion of his right drives the knife all the way in and turns it back and forth and here you can see his ability because if he's good the first flow of black blood shouldn't splash out of the pot and secondly if the blow is properly delivered the hog loses all of its strength in one great shudder that jolts its entire body and its squealing immediately drops in pitch even though the butchers don't want it to stop completely because with the gasps of its death rattle the blood gushes better, once the animal is dead they wipe the knife on its bristles and then tie the four legs and while two or three of them lift it up the others turn the tub right side up and then the animal is lowered inside it and untied, at this point the steaming water arrives in big kettles each carried by two men using a pole placed under the handle, the head butcher takes a dipper and pours a little water on the skin of the lifeless animal to see if the water is hot enough and in fact if it's sufficiently scalding the hog's bristles and outer skin should come away with a simple tug of the fingers, if the

15

test works they pour all the water into the tub submerging all but a small part of the hog and they scrape that part with their knives and then they keep turning the animal over and over while they strip the hide and even when they get to the feet they use hooks to remove the soft white crunchy cartilage that covers the inside bone of the hooves then four of them lift the animal and hang it from the gallows set up by the owner passing the rope under the tendons of the hind legs which are spread as much as possible and then with a hatchet they chop it from top to bottom I mean from the rear end to the mouth and when they hit a bone they don't go around it but cut right through even using wedges and a mallet, when this operation is over two equal and symmetrical halves of the hog hang there from which the blood drips in long streaks for a good quarter of an hour until after being repeatedly doused with cold water the flesh is nice and clean red and white and to find out how much there is all you have to do is weigh one half because the other is absolutely identical, then the two portions are laid on sloping planks while all the relatives gather to make salami with the lean meat cotechino with the fatty part morette with the cooked blood and saltimbronze with the more pungent meat, while the rest is put in cold storage and covered with salt, and to let the relatives know that everything is ready for this operation you just send one of the kids around to take a cutlet to each family and you can be sure that in due course you'll get one back just as big except not from the priest or the landowners who never reciprocate. This profession of hog butcher is a hereditary one transmitted from father to son and now after such a long association with pigs these men even have faces that look like them with ears that stick out and flop over a little and squarish noses with horizontal nostrils that dilate and contract with every breath, sewing the eyes of broody hens is another profession that's always been exclusive, this one to the women of a single family I mean the Penar women, the Penars live in a wooden house that sprouts mushrooms after every rainstorm and no one goes over their way because there's practically no path leading to their house and you can get there only through the culverts of various landowners so that strictly speaking the Penars don't even have the right of access to their home, every so often some hen having laid an egg doesn't get up and go away cackling and clucking but stays sitting on top of it in total and loving immobility as though dead as a doornail and you can see she's alive by staring for a while at her round eye with its black pupil surrounded by a little red circle if you have the patience to wait for about ten minutes you can see the eye closing and reopening like a camera lens with such rapidity that the movement is almost imperceptible, the hen doesn't care about food or air or how much time goes by and the next day she's still there with her comb a little ashen and what that means is that she's becoming a broody hen and has to be set to brood, and so the women go around to other families swapping unfertilized eggs for good ones, the unfertilized eggs are from hens that have no rooster except for those silly little bantams that instead of spending time with them are always fighting among themselves pecking each other's combs and then running around splashing blood all over the chicken yard, justice in the henhouse is very much a question of luck and scenes take place that can only be compared with human politics, for example roosters and hens all standing ridiculously in utter silence with necks straight up and eyes motionless suddenly one hen gives another one a sharp peck and it's obvious to all present that the second one has suffered an injustice and has therefore acquired the right to give just as sharp a peck in her turn to another one and this third hen has no right to object because all that's happened is simply a just revenge as you can tell by the raucous and universal cry of approval by which the congress of bystanders authorizes the three protagonists to disperse and resume their regular lives, so when the women have collected a sufficient number of good eggs they go home and put them under the broody hen spreading her wings so that the entire mound is well covered and kept warm, from that moment on the hen won't be disturbed again except to inspect the eggs after the first days of nesting when by holding them up to the light it's possible to see a kind of shadowy thread inside which means that a chick is being formed, then when the chicks hatch there must always be a child standing by because as long as the chicks are all yellow the hen puts up with their pecking and scratching and even lets them walk on her comb, but if by chance a shell cracks and an unlucky black chick pokes its eye and neck out right away the mother

18

makes an irritated and guttural sound and ruffles her
feathers and quivers and with a peck thrusts it back in
the shell with the obvious intention of restoring it to
nature, and here before she pecks a hole in its head the
child must intervene with a glass of strong spirits and
dunk the hen's head in it up to the eyes so that by
inhaling she gets drunk because this is the only way to
keep her from being able to distinguish the black chick
from the others and thus to allow it the luxury of being
born, but inebriation is only a temporary remedy and
since you can't always be there to reinforce the liquor
fumes the minute they evaporate this is what makes the
work of the Penar women invaluable they being special-
ists in sewing the broody hen's eyes with needle and
fine thread here the skill lies in piercing the eyelids not
at the edge but a little bit higher that is to say just above
certain tough little nerves in such a way that they don't
break when the hen tries to open her eyes, and at the
same time there's no need for the eye to be completely
closed enough of a peephole has to be left so that she
can orient herself when walking around with her chicks
but not enough to be able to tell the white ones from that
black one which by the way ever since the first day of its
life has consciously learned to keep a certain distance
from its mother. The operation performed by the Penar
women is also necessary when the brood consists partly
of chicks and partly of ducklings, it may happen that the
ducklings are the same pale yellow color as their chicken
brothers and sisters and so at first all goes well but
trouble starts after the first rain when the hen goes

strutting off with her little ones to divide up in equal portions the worms that have been driven out of the water and gets all ruffled and upset when she sees some of her children dive contrary to nature into puddles where they bob around more lively than ever as though congratulating each other, and after a moment's dismay she realizes they're not of her race and off she goes with the others leaving them to their fate, so that's why the sewing done by the Penar women is the ideal remedy, during the operation the hen drools from her open beak with her tongue sticking out sideways and has a sweet dazed look that comes close to beatitude.

The heart of the village is the tavern and not the church because strange to say the church which goes all the way back to the thirteenth century is located on the other side of the river which more or less constitutes the boundary line of our province, and already the fact that to go to church you have to cross the bridge and practically enter another province bothers the peasants a little since it's only in their own place that they feel at ease take for example a drunkard in his own house he can create an uproar and break the dishes while at your house he stands in the doorway behaving himself with a stupid smile of submission or rests his buttocks on the edge of the chair so that one push and he'd slide off on the floor, there's no public square in front of the tavern and it sometimes happens that strangers even ask you as they go by which is the road that leads to our village and you tell them the village is here and they ask you what do you mean here and you repeat here and of

course you point God knows why to the tavern, the
tavern is the meeting place for our fellows after supper
they all come on bicycles with no lights and if it's
pitch-dark as happens all too often in winter all you
have to do to ride properly is keep to the right on the
road with your face looking up toward the treetops since
it's never so dark that the trees aren't darker than the
sky, and if there's actually a fog so thick that you
swallow it in mouthfuls and it gets all mixed up with the
wine then you'd better ride with the wheel of the bicycle
hugging the edge of the grass and you can be sure you
won't end up in the ditch, getting around in the dark is
so much a matter of practice that the Albino our village
blind man always walks with his chin up and with his
cane probes and follows the line between the road and
the grass of the ditch and since his hearing is very sharp
and he pauses the minute he hears a noise he'd never
run into any danger if the kids of the Mill district didn't
deliberately stop right in front of him in total silence
with their bicycles then to be sure the Albino takes a
tumble but he gets up flailing so hard with his cane you
can hear it whistle in the air. In the Mill district, just
across the river, stands the church where the women are
kept separate from the men and when a stranger who
doesn't know this custom turns up in our church and
pretending to be innocent gets in among the women the
girls immediately move away from him and the men
turn to look at this mangy dog and the priest stops
saying mass and turning around from the altar tells him
to join the men if he's a man and he's about to faint with

21

shame and joins the men but close to the door and at the first opportunity he makes his escape and we can be sure he'll never come back and all our men with a nod of their heads express their pride in our priest and the mass resumes in a very elevated and contented atmosphere and the village boys who are with the men and therefore are men are proud that the girls have witnessed the scene because certainly that fellow had come deliberately for the purpose of setting his eyes on one of our girls and that means he was someone from Marega those guys from Marega have a lot of nerve and think they can go looking for girls in other people's villages even picking out a pretty one when already there's a boy there on the spot who's been thinking about her for years and so one evening the boys in our village got together and waited on the bridge with sticks for the ones from Marega and when they arrived all hell broke loose and they jumped off their bicycles befuddled and amazed as though they didn't know where they were and meanwhile like fools they were getting the bejesus beat out of them and their bicycles went flying into the river which is deep right there until they turned tail and ran with their hands on their heads to protect themselves from the volley of stones.

2. *The Devil's foot*

Every girl in the village has to be careful not to spend her time with boys except on Monday Wednesday or Friday which are open days when being with someone doesn't mean anything while on other days in everyone's eyes it would mean they were sweethearts and then the boy would no longer have the right to look at anyone else unless he wanted to get beaten up, he must carry on the courtship one stage at a time first letting himself be seen with the girl in the stretch of road leading from the church to her house, after a couple of weeks lingering with her at the gate and then a few weeks later going into the house after which a breakup is inconceivable because the honor of the whole family has been pledged and if the girl has brothers they'll make a point of finding out every evening if the relationship is going as it should, this tradition naturally has its drawbacks and its most delicate moment comes when for the first time a couple is seen together on a proper day, from then on she's no longer free in the eyes of the other boys and so if by chance she has no wish to get engaged right away or is waiting for someone who's a soldier or someone who's now going with another girl but doesn't go inside her house and therefore might still break things off, then she can resort to a small stratagem that is always going to and from mass in the company of one or more girl friends so that if some boy joins them nobody knows officially whether he's doing it for one girl or another and this business of girls going around the village in small groups is a custom by now also for the reason that everybody looks at a beautiful girl and so by becoming her friend another girl can get into circulation and it's easier for her to find a sweetheart, as a result these little groups of girls always contain a very beautiful one who makes all the decisions and three or four homely ones who carry out her wishes.

Once in a while I'd happen to see my sister Narcisa coming back from mass or other church functions with the Duckling or the little Mouse and even sometimes with Tonia Bojon but it didn't occur to me that the time had come when my sister too would be engaging in little subterfuges in order to be with boys without however feeling involved with any of them, and besides the Ducks and the Mice are our neighbors and we're slightly related to the Bojons and for every ten times you go to the village if only to buy salt you're likely to come back five times with one of the Bojon kids since there are thirteen of them and at home they never know what to do and have everything in common even their beds and clothes so when one of them comes back from early mass he takes off his Sunday best and lends it to one of his brothers who that way is able to go to the second mass and this is another reason why it's hard to tell them apart, then in the evening those who are the first to go to bed take over the double bed and the others make do with the stable, the ideal thing is to stay awake as long as possible playing cards keeping in mind the risk of not being able to find a place in the double bed and so at a certain hour when only a few of the brothers are left they send one of them to reconnoiter and feel to see if the bed is full because in that case they might as well get out another candle or more carbide and go on with their card game, feeling around the bed is a delicate operation because you never know in which direction the sleepers have put their feet and which their heads and if by chance you put your hand on someone's face there's the danger that you'll get bitten, not all the Bojons are healthy specimens in fact one of the older brothers has one leg as short as a newborn baby's and therefore walks with crutches and when he falls down he can't get up which is why the Bojons who have no toilet and like everybody else do their business in the ditches that surround the house have tied ropes to the trees in the middle of which the paralytic usually relieves himself so that when he's finished he can get up again, once however the rope broke and only much later was it possible to help the poor devil because instead of yelling and calling for help crazy as he is he started laughing first to himself then louder and louder so that even if someone had heard him he wouldn't have paid any attention thinking he was just having his usual orgasm as would happen every time he found himself half naked but finally he tried to grab hold of the rope and get up but couldn't do it then he started whimpering like an ox with the chills and the first kid who heard him thought it was too funny a scene to keep to himself so he went to call a friend and then some more friends and then the crazy man's brothers and to make a long story short the crazy man was still there naked and rolling around in his own excrement surrounded by some twenty people when his mother came out and pulled him up kissing and caressing him and wiping the filth off him with leaves, to cure her paralytic son la Bojona even took him to Padre Pio hoping to wring a miracle out of him, the friar was in church wearing his cowl and walking with his hands in a pair of gloves dragging one foot and spitting with a grim look on his face and a bitter mouth as though he'd been chewing tobacco and just as la Bojona opened the door and came in propping up her son on his crutches the friar was actually muttering as he spat haugh haugh you old hag which made la Bojona poor thing start turning the paralytic around so as to retreat ashamed of being recognized so quickly, but the friar wasn't talking to her he was talking to another woman tiny hunchbacked and swathed in black who was making ugly faces on her way out, as soon as she realized her mistake la Bojona retraced her steps tidying up her son's clothes pushing him and shouting at him to make him turn around again he however was now starting to act up both because of the trip whose purpose he didn't understand and for being constantly pushed this way and that and with his eyes bulging from his head he was already brandishing his crutches at his mother like a club and the more she smiled and encouraged him the more he slavered and raged, the friar already standing with one foot on the step of another door was observing them out of the corner of his eye undecided whether to leave or come back for this misshapen pair, finally the paralytic calmed down a little and put down his crutches though he still kept looking suspiciously at his mother who meanwhile was reknotting her black kerchief under her chin and making an effort to recover her toothless mouth from under the wrinkles and folds into which it was generally sucked back disappearing in the empty space as though she didn't even have one and she was smiling at the friar so that he'd come back meanwhile patting the shoulder of her placated and taciturn son with her hand the way a peasant at the market does with his ox when he wants to show that it won't try to gore anyone, the friar too was adjusting his cowl so that now his face was wholly invisible and with hands joined he walked slowly looking at the floor and entered a confessional, la Bojona abandoned her son crouched there on the tiles and knelt at the confessional starting off by saying pio pio pio padre and padre pio and then a torrent of words, the friar listened in silence and then said he couldn't, he didn't have the power and that having the power to heal was less important than having the strength to endure, the old woman was contemplating that talking cowl through the holes in the grating and already she'd forgotten it all and was no longer asking for anything and at a certain point when neither of them was speaking she broke the silence by asking where is my dead son, her firstborn in fact had died on her six years

27

before while working on the beams of a house under construction, a fire had broken out and the man had taken refuge on the farthest beam and sat huddled there at the very end of it and he was the last thing they saw disappear in the flames, and afterwards la Bojona could no longer see anything for the way he lay flopping back and forth in the middle of the dusty yard like a wounded crow stripped of its feathers that sweeps the ground for half an hour before succumbing to the kids aiming their stones at its little skull and then finally it lies there spread out and gasping with its round eye wide open and gall trickling from its beak, and so in the end the old woman fell prostrate twitching rhythmically because it was the beating of her heart that moved her, and lying there she kept moaning uhu uhu, just like that, blowing away the dirt and on the floor she had cleaned this way she drooled a little from the mouth, the friar answered pray for him that he expiate the last of the seven sins, then he emerged from the confessional passed with his cassock next to the paralytic who was morosely observing his bare feet, the mother again kneeling there deep in thought was carried away in spirit and saw a miraculous apparition, her dead son still clinging to the beam in the middle of the fire as at the moment of his passage from this world to the next, and then she understood that it was no longer her son's body but his soul, which being without mortal sin believed it could fly directly out of the fire but it was mistaken because it had no wings and fell into the flames getting scorched all over and expiating the sin of pride, with great difficulty the

28

son was able to climb back up onto whatever burning
ruins were still standing and balance himself once more
on the beam while hell took shape below him and
serpents of fire with poisonous flickering tongues could
be seen among the flames, in the second year the son
felt his wings sprout and took flight but after barely a
meter he felt himself engulfed by the fiery abyss while
the serpents moved forward the better to get at him,
amid great torment the son succeeded again after many
months in climbing up the wall and perching on his
beam, and so every year he made the mistake of flying
since it seemed to him that his wings were fully developed, by now many years had gone by and examining
him closely his mother saw that he had very broad white
wings between which his little legs and tiny head almost
disappeared and with the next flight he would surely
rise all the way into the skies, but the advice that his
mother heard herself giving him with due solicitude was
that he should wait several more years before risking it
again, because after all he wasn't so badly off there on
that beam, and that rather than departing too soon and
falling once more into the fire it was better to wait even
for too long until the others came to call him, that that
would be the infallible guarantee that the time had
come, and that if she were in his shoes she'd be content
to stay sitting there comfortably on the beam even for all
eternity, and in saying this the old woman strained
forward to speak toward the beyond where her son's
tiny head almost lost between his big wings seemed to
understand and nod yes, and nod yes, smile and nod

29

yes, this vision lasted only for the time it took Padre Pio to cross the church and leave and when she came to her senses the woman was just in time to see the friar open the door and disappear, open the door and disappear, open the door, disappear, and so she returned home in the train completely consoled with her son's bundle stashed in a corner on the floor of the carriage.

Anyway I didn't suspect anything when I'd see Narcisa always coming back with a group even from the triduums, triduums are often held in the spring when we need rain and instead the sun beats down and scorches the grass and then all the people go each evening for three evenings in procession through the fields following the priest who with careful gestures blesses the crosses nailed to the trees and in chorus with the frogs whose skin is cracked by the heat intone persistent litanies calling for rain, in spring a little before Easter Don Panzetta also organizes the blessing of the eggs which means that each family prepares a little altar in front of its door a small table covered with a cloth and on it the saint who on various occasions has turned out to be the most effective that is to say Saint Anthony or Saint Dorotea who is the patron saint of the village or even Saint Bovo who cures hoof-and-mouth disease and in front of the saint they put a basket with the eggs which the priest blesses and the bell ringer coming along behind collects them and if by chance the family wants to keep a few of the blessed eggs for itself it must prepare another basket no larger than the first so as not to display bad manners in front of the priest, it's always a good idea to keep some blessed eggs in the sideboard in case of illness in fact misers who have no eggs because they have no hens are always full of ailments, by going to the triduums a girl is more likely to meet a boy who has a few fields of his own as proper social ambition would require, since obviously anyone who has no land has no interest in invoking rain which would then give him rheumatism for nothing, so that's the reason why all the aristocratic youth of the village go to the triduums the girls with white complexions not burned by the sun perfumed walking erect and nicely dressed and their breasts stand out and aren't squashed against their chests and they have soft eyes that when necessary in the middle of the throng on feast days know how to close if the sun is too strong, the boys who own bicycles and shirts and move slowly and majestically accustomed to driving mules or oxen and not working in place of the oxen like for example Bepi Temeno, the Temenos are poor people who sweat blood and go to work as field hands and the landowners make them do the heaviest work like for example digging wells, to dig a well you must first make the hole for the first cylinder and then the man gets inside the cylinder and goes on digging underneath so that the cylinder keeps dropping down and when it's dropped its whole length the men outside set another one on top of it without any danger to the digger because the cylinders are the same diameter and can't go inside one another, the trouble starts when they run into water at the depth foreseen with the watch, to detect water with a watch

31

the dowser smears his wrists with grease and walks around with his arms outstretched so as to catch the emanations of underground moisture and finally he stops on the chosen spot takes out his watch and holding it by the chain stands there with his legs spread and head bowed staring at the ground and then the watch moves like a pendulum and swings as many times as the number of meters of depth for the spring of water or rather not exactly meters but a little more or a little less depending on the nature of the soil, there's another method in which you can actually do without the watch holding instead a curved green branch between your hands but for this second method you need special men whose nerves are sensitive to water and in our village there aren't any, so when the digger reaches the spring he must still go on digging until the water flows abundantly and then the well is good otherwise it could dry up with the first sun, to work in the water they could use rubber boots but the fact is they don't keep you warm and standing for weeks on end in the liquid mud you suffer from the cold all the same so you might as well do without boots and save the expense, and that's why old Temeno came down with a lot of illnesses and now his poor wife takes him around on a cart made with an axle set between two bicycle wheels between which the man is encased like a dish of polenta, even now the Temenos go from one village to another to dig wells or scythe by hand using a reaper's scythe the kind where you swing your whole body so that when poor Bepi goes to the tavern after a day's work he walks swinging his ass from side to side as if he were still scything and you can see from a mile away that he doesn't own a thing in this world and therefore the girls don't even look at him besides he's realized that nothing can be done about it and is satisfied to drink and at the most play cards, anyway at a certain moment I realized that after dinner Narcisa would take a straw from the broom cut it up and make herself a bunch of toothpicks with which she'd carefully clean her teeth one by one then she'd go to her room which is over the kitchen and through the holes in the floor I could see that she'd lighted a candle or the acetylene lamp and put it at the window but I didn't realize it was a signal to show she was ready at a certain point she'd put out all the lights I thought she'd gone to bed instead she'd come down the stairs with her hair all combed wearing on her head a shawl that I'd never seen because it came from my mother's dowry and then powdered and perfumed she'd go out the back door and stand at the gateway talking with someone who spoke in a low voice keeping his head down on the handlebars of his bicycle so that not even by passing close was it possible to recognize him, this habit of keeping his head down bothered my brother and also my mother as far as I was concerned it was because the boy was shy but my mother said that way over there by the gate they could fall into temptation and at this point my brother's jaws would start grinding with anger and he'd go out the door and stand on the stoop tall and dark with legs spread and say hey hey and then you saw the boy raise his head and Narcisa turn around trembling and he went back inside while they cool as could be came pushing the bicycle under the kitchen window there within earshot so that if you wanted to you could have put your ear to the window and heard everything they were saying I don't say that anyone did but to be reassured that they weren't doing anything wrong it was enough for them to know that we could check up on them at any moment, they went on behaving like sweethearts outside there in the open which is the right thing to do before getting engaged even when the weather was bad only if it rained or a strong wind was blowing you could hear that they'd moved from the front wall to the side wall both because there they were protected from the gusts of rain and because that's the wall through which the chimney passes and it's always warm and by putting your palms against the bricks you can warm your hands or else by leaning right against the wall with your shoulders you can feel the warmth penetrating all the way to the lungs and dislodging phlegm that you can then spit out in mouthfuls, even the birds had become aware of this supply of warmth in winter when branches and grass are stiff with frost and the cold is so piercing it freezes the water that seeps into the trees and when you go through the open country-side with your shotgun following the tracks of a hare which you can tell from those of a dog because they're much thinner and the points of the claws are placed differently, if you're tired and stop to clean off the icicles that have formed around your eyelashes and which are nothing but your own immediately frozen breath and if you keep listening with a little patience you may hear all of a sudden something like a long cracking sound it's some tree that's been split by the ice but the ice itself still holds it upright and together there's no danger of its falling and in fact even the blackbird that was sleeping in a hole and had got jolted out flies up only a couple of feet and then makes a nose dive back into its lair, but the birds that decide to spend the night in the tiny holes or on the nails driven in the wall of the chimney know they're risking their skins because all it takes is for someone to open the shutters and slam them suddenly against the wall to crush them by the dozen and in fact there's always someone smart enough to drive nails deliberately into the outside of the chimney and by this method to be assured of a convenient supply of little roasted birds with crunchy but to tell the truth rather bitter bones because sparrows are too small to make it worth the trouble to cut them open and clean them and so they get eaten in one bite along with whatever they have in their stomachs and craws, so Narcisa was playing sweethearts under the kitchen window and nobody in the village could have anything to say about it and the dangerous time in which something might have happened went by in this way and finally her boyfriend presented himself inside the house as well and from that moment on he was like one of the family and had a chair reserved for him in a corner of the kitchen next to the fireplace where my mother could watch him out of the corner of her eye while she was

35

knitting and scratching her head with her knitting needles, and now no one could approach Narcisa and pinch her with impunity except on the night of Epiphany when we make *brugnèli*, these are big bonfires and each district makes its own by collecting bundles of wood and cornstalks that haven't got damp, these bundles are stacked vertically around a pole and tied with wire so as to form a cone about seven or eight meters high and about three or four meters at the base of course far from any barns and haystacks that might catch fire, for this reason we put our *brugnèlo* right in the middle of the crossings and as it gets dark young men disguised as fat-assed old witches come through the culverts and assemble there imitating the Italian language and babbling all sorts of nonsense and indecent sayings protected by the immunity that rhymes enjoy on these occasions they go in and out of the surrounding houses just as they please and while rubbing soot on the cheeks and necks of the girls their hands explore still further inside dresses left ready to be opened they take the opportunity to feel if the girl has firm tits and next day the word gets around and they get together to bring the list of eligible girls up to date, assuming nothing worse happens like the time three of them kidnapped the little Flea taking advantage of the fact that her family lives isolated in the middle of the swamp where there's never another living soul and they carried her screaming to the heavens to the Fisherman's hut and four hours later gave her back to the night and this is the reason why she's still unmarried because nobody wants her except Joàca the cripple, having been smeared with soot the girls take care not to wash it off but go to the bonfire with dirty faces because when the fire is lighted and the huge flames rouse people out of their houses and make them assemble outside, then in the crowd thronging around the fire to look at the masked figures who jump on the burning bundles or climb up the pole right in the middle of the blaze while someone splashes them with pails of water so that they don't catch on fire, the girls enjoy showing that they've been marked in fact even the homely ones whom no one's looked at go off by themselves in the shadows and embellish themselves with soot.

A monotonous sequence of days and evenings with no signs of danger then brought us to the eve of the wedding and at this point the bride's family by which I mean ours had to shoulder the burden of a complicated operation and there was great confusion, my brother took it on himself to find a cook by asking the last family who had had a wedding and in this way getting the address of one who lived in the village of Merlara and was a specialist in organizing and conducting wedding banquets he had been the one to provide the food when the Fornasari and Pigozzi wedding had taken place at home la Pigozza was one of the most beautiful girls in the village firm and solid and upright as a poplar she'd toss her head like a mare making her shining fluid mane ripple and like Narcisa she too was always so clean that it was impossible to find a single speck of dirt on her and she didn't even seem to be the daughter of her mother who when she worked in the fields had the bad habit of not going to the ditch to piss which after all was pretty far away but doing it right there in the midst of the other field hands she'd piss standing up with her legs spread and her full-length skirts hiding it all so that you heard the water trickling on the ground but didn't see anything except the puddle after the woman had moved on, it's obvious of course that to enjoy this convenience you have to give up wearing underdrawers, a self-respecting cook however has his professional dignity and doesn't tell you yes I'm coming right away but waits until he's made inquiries about the family whether or not it's able to pay for a wedding feast that's truly a wedding feast and so my brother had to return home very downcast in his proprietary pride for having to submit to the decision of this outsider and thinking in his heart that the outsider could even go you know where that he'd arrange things by replacing him with la Pegnatta for the roast capons and veal la Moschetta for the smoked risotto and la Piandotta for the broth and tortellini, or better still by taking the uncooked veal and chickens and cake flour to some restaurant in the province of Verona which wouldn't be all that far away and give orders to the waiters to make it their business to deliver the whole thing to us crisp and piping hot at exactly eleven o'clock on the Saturday of the wedding when people would be starting to arrive and sitting down at the table, but on that same afternoon along comes the cook looking as though he owned the place and he plants himself there in our yard without even greeting us gazing this way and that with the air of an expert and at this point our esteem for him as we stand around him grows beyond all bounds and my brother respects but hates him and his gorge rises so much that he starts grinding his jaws waiting for the man to make up his mind and even my sister who after all is the one most concerned comes to the upstairs window and waits for the outsider's decision and the outsider finally decides yes saying he'll take it on and he sits down on the ground and we all gather around him and he takes pencil and paper asking for the number of guests and gets mad when he hears it can't be figured for certain because we don't know if just one person is coming from each family or two or three and then there are always those who come without being invited so that the hypothetical number that can be suggested beforehand may turn out to be three times as many the cook at this point begins his calculations and sets the number of capons and how many kilos of beef and the number of geese but here he has to make a correction because we don't have any geese however as compensation we do have guinea hens only a few of which by now are left and we'd all be glad to get rid of the guinea hens because they're haughty creatures that don't sleep in the chicken house but as high as they can get under the bright stars so that to deal with this natural inclination of theirs my father has had to build a kind of lattice of poles suspending it like a hammock between two Canadian poplars some thirty yards away from the house and when it gets dark the guinea hens flap up onto it heavily and stay curled up there until the light of dawn pierces the thin membranes of their eyelids and strikes the pupil, then the first one to awaken flies away shaking the whole wooden contraption so that the others are catapulted in midair and must helter-skelter, on pain of death, wake up orient themselves break their fall and glide off somewhere, what throws this passable but not very ingenious system into turmoil is the full moon because it wakes the poor creatures up at the wrong time when the gears of their little brains are still enmeshed in sleep and their dimmed eyes see things confusedly, what happens is that the poor birds fly off in compact flocks and bash themselves headlong against the side of the house with the result that in the morning we always find a battered heap of them under the windows, the cook takes note of the fact that we can substitute guinea hens for geese but obviously we need twice as many because a goose is equivalent to two guinea hens and he also establishes the quantity and types of cheese and the number and weight of the cakes and therefore the number of eggs required taking into account that eggs also go in the tortellini which follow the broth and precede the risotto, the wine is brought out at that moment as are the peppers onions and tomato, of course one eats only the best part of the poultry and not for example the claws which get thrown away and the heads and necks which the cook takes home with him in a basket, the cooking should be done the day before the meal the pasta and cakes too but anyway the outdoor oven has to be got ready right away a rather high one because the meat stuck on spits has to be cooked far from the flame and the polenta gets browned on the grill over the fire and as it roasts it forms a skin on the surface that soaks up all the fat dripping down from the animals, there won't be any bread because it's complicated to make, although in the village there's an oven built by the Drugottis in which those who want to can bake bread, first reserving it in advance so as to have the whole day at their disposal and make enough batches to last a month, without having to give money to the owner who pays himself by coming to count the loaves and keeping one out of ten, I'd eaten bread a few times and remembered that what I liked best was the smell that when the storage bin is filled spreads throughout the kitchen and whets your appetite but it must be a smell that also appeals to ants because after the bread had been in the bin for a week we noticed with astonishment that it was swarming with big and little ants coming from God knows where, that's no reason to throw the bread away because actually as my mother said ants are very clean creatures not like cockchafers which, when you have your food taken to you in the fields, fall right into your bowl of soup and they're disgusting because they're always mating, anyway even if ants are clean it was still a nuisance to eat old bread because first you had to inspect it carefully even in the holes and you could never be sure that there weren't a few nests of ants inside that by running around in your mouth could make your tonsils itch, maybe that's why the oven gets used less and less and for whole months can be said to be completely abandoned like the time it became a lair of martens and weasels and they set about devouring chicks and cockerels inside it leaving as slender evidence a few stray feathers until the Drugottis realized what was happening and collecting a bunch of old shoes and broken-down boots flushed them out with the smell of burning leather and the minute they appeared at the door of the oven ready to jump down they shot them dead on the spot and if no one had got them out of there they'd still be inside rotting and putrefied, so no bread anyway the browned polenta is every bit as good as bread and it gets even better if then it's cooked on the dripping pan the way we do and again still better if it's got beans in it I mean if it's full of black beans which during the cooking stay whole like pieces of candied fruit and when chewed explode a sweet-tasting flour in the mouth so it can very well be eaten with bread because the fact is that when you eat polenta with beans you don't eat anything else.

Narcisa was never present during the great preparations and not even when her fiancé came with his mule and cart did she come down to check that all her things were being loaded, my mother had to attend to it, and during these operations I stared wide-eyed at the sight of large many-colored tablecloths with bows dangling from the edges passing in front of me things we hadn't bought and that we didn't know we had in the house they came from my mother's dowry and had been hidden away for more than twenty years and now here they emerged in the sunlight for the space of a day

because my sister was becoming a bride she would stick
them back in some storage chest so as to hand them on
to her daughters, dresses were loaded on the cart and
sheets and mattresses and hats some of them half a
century old with wide black brims maybe the trousseau
of that great-grandmother who had been a nun before
getting married, as my mother had been too but she'd
left the convent because it wasn't good for her health
still she'd always remained somewhat of a nun and the
only fairy tales she was able to tell us around the hearth
when the snow covered the windows were the lives of
the saints, the captain having gone back inside the
unbelievers dragged the saint out of the captain's door
he stood there all alone among the ruffians barefoot
with his buttons undone like this and there was such a
crowd it was hard to see him and the people said don't
die and he hardly answered and only out of pure
necessity and seldom raising his head and when they
approached the pyre there was a great outcry there's the
pyre abjure and live and he answered more steadfastly
than ever, and when they arrived at the pyre the police
made the people draw back and to frighten him they
made smoke rise several times and many were frightened but he remained firm even though one of the Ten
was there ready with a horse to take him back home if
he abjured and after the smoke they lit the fire and the
living man vanished and the dead one fell out, every
evening our mother warned us against playing with
Zaira who was one of the girls who most often would
get boys to remove her splinters, you ought to know

that when someone gets a little piece of glass or some other kind of splinter in his bare foot he doesn't have to go home and get a needle the little tip that's still inside can very well be removed by using a Christ's-thorn which is hard and five inches long, this is an operation that boys are very wiling to perform on girls because to get ready for it the girl has to lie down on the ground and when she raises her foot you can see everything, for this reason some girls deliberately pretend to limp when playing and they get surrounded by a swarm of boys saying get a thorn and the girl lies down and lifts her foot and enjoys seeing them all crowding around fighting for the place from where they can see best, and these are the things that infuriate Panzetta and make him stamp his feet loudly when he comes to hear of them during confession. There was a week when confessions were made every evening and to be exact it was the time when a movie van turned up in our village, the scenes they showed didn't form a complete film but were a series of half reels the posters however were promising because in one photograph you saw a woman with bare legs who was hiding her thing with her hands but in doing so she was bending forward with the result that she also showed her tits, this woman knew very well what she was doing and she was doing it quite deliberately because her mouth was set in an expression of false wonder and all things considered of beckoning satisfaction, naturally the whole crowd that gathered in the cinema was eagerly awaiting the moment when the woman would appear and indeed she did appear but simultaneously the whole film became yellow and full of spots as though they were showing a violent rainstorm it was obviously a reel much consumed by use, for all we know it had played in all the villages in the Veneto before coming to us, the woman was white as could be and her mouth black as could be and her eyes kept moving like those of people born and brought up in the city usually do because, as my father says sympathetically, they have to be on their guard against constant dangers, her legs were just right with well-shaped ankles and trim calves and the thighs up above were firm and rounded and perfectly proportioned, I'd never seen a woman with bare legs like this but I understood immediately as though I had known all along that this was the way a woman should be formed and that after all she's completely different from us males and that any part of her whatsoever is exciting and desirable, everybody else must have thought and felt the same thing because all the rows in the cinema began violently rocking back and forth, some began to squirm with not only their eyes wide open but their mouths as well and when the actress leaned forward pursing her lips in that surly and condescending way promised on the posters and in the space revealed by her light dress you saw the swaying of her two breasts the apocalyptic silence of the audience was broken by yelps of desire for which each of us felt responsible, I felt the blood pounding in my head like a hammer and my heart was beating so hard that I heard its reverberation and not only my body was trembling but even the wooden chair on which I was sitting and my eyesight dimmed but there were some even worse off than I like the one who carried away by his orgasm at a certain moment flung himself on the row of chairs in front of him and at this point no one was sitting still any longer the seats kept creaking one man stood up then everybody the canvas tent began swaying it felt suffocating by now the woman had disappeared but all of us had her legs engraved far behind the pupils of our eyes no one was looking at anyone else not one of us would have suspected for a thousand years that the female figure was so well formed to get a breath of air someone unfastened the iron stakes of the tent and crawled outside on all fours immediately everybody unhooked the canvas and slunk away with the bloody and stupefied look of the bull whose brain is stunned from having been hit on the head with a sledgehammer but it was useless to try to wriggle out of it because during the next day and all the following week Panzetta sought us out in our homes and one by one we all confessed and in order to get to the church we had to pass the meadow where the movie tent had stood and the only traces of it that remained were a few holes in the ground and a trampled expanse of heel prints as though the goat-footed Devil had sprung up out of the depths and danced there with all his following.

Enclosures. On sanctity

The news of la Bojona's miraculous vision is known to the whole village because ever since the poor woman's

skull was crushed by her paralytic son with a blow of his
crutch documents have been collected in our village to
promote the process of her beatification, having returned home from her meeting with Padre Pio she had
come to consider any attempt to cure her son as a sin
and she kept him always beside her placing herself at
his service always smiling and caressing and when her
son sat on the ground his chest and neck upright and all
his faculties excited except his legs like a spring nailed at
one of its ends to a plank and flailed wildly about with
his crutches the mother didn't move away but crept
under that umbrella of hailstones until she was able to
stroke her aroused son lightly with her hand and
murmur to him naughty boy and every Sunday she led
him to the first mass and however early you might get
up to go to the fields it was never so early that you
didn't notice in front of you on the path dampened by
the fog the holes left by a pair of crutches and a pair of
heels and at home she always kept him in the same
room with her and if the doctor came she hid him in
order to show her total contempt for science and since
our doctor is also a painter and makes his rounds to visit
his patients with his easel tied to the handlebars of his
bicycle and between one visit and another always finds
the inspiration to sketch the outlines of a nice landscape
picture on those days when inspiration came to him in
the middle of the Bojon copse and he'd set up his
contraption there and brush away to the amazement of
cats and turkeys whistling softly in various keys depending on the colors it struck his fancy to use on those

47

days la Bojona confined her son to a small room and stayed there in the dark to keep him company with the windows closed so that the doctor wouldn't examine him and sinfully try to cure him, only on the day when her son brought his crutch down on her head and she herself heard the bone in her skull crack as she croaked did she make a sudden face between fright and reproach but immediately repented of it and smiled and died, Julia Imbroja set out to gather evidence of la Bojona's sanctity and in a short while filled a notebook which the priest refused to include among the parish documents and which Julia Imbroja always keeps in her bosom between one and another of the numerous black chemises she wears and wandering through the village square she waits patiently for a cart driver from some other village passing under the ivy of the tavern to get thirsty and stop his cart and tie up his mule and go in and order a flask of wine, then she goes after him smiling broadly and spraying saliva right and left and standing in front of the man who is half dozing from his journey she takes out the notebook and reads him one after another with dramatic emphasis the documents and depositions that sooner or later will end up in the history books of the Church, the first of the documents is an autobiographical note by the saint herself compiled at the request of la Imbroja who with great farsightedness had for years been constructing a saint for our village, the text began LIFE OF AGATA BOGGION WRITTEN BY HERSELF AND CONSIGNED TO GIULIA FORNARO BROGGIO AND COPIED BY HER AS

HERE WRITTEN and continued summarized for convenience in the third person: that finding herself to have a paralytic son, how he ordered her to light a small fire, but it didn't seem to him well lit and so he hit her, once he wanted her to put her hands in the fire and she put them in and she heard Saint Dorotea who came fluttering down from heaven in a beautiful light holding a scale and said to her put yourself here and she ran to put herself on the scale and a dove burst out of the cloud and alighted on the other pan of the scale going pio pio pio pio so that she'd go to Padre Pio and indeed she went and understood things that it's best to keep silent about, and when she came back she said to the family look at this unfortunate boy who looks like the prodigal son in his ragged clothes from now on he'll no longer be put aside but treated as the favorite son, now hear the testimonies: the undersigned Zarvello attests in good faith that when he went into the church to hear mass at the moment the priest was raising the chalice the saint in some way whether seated or kneeling levitated herself from the floor remaining suspended and the non-believers, at this point measuring the stranger up and down, were able to pass their hands under the legs of the chair to the great astonishment of those present, and the undersigned Passacantando through his deceased mother has preserved the memory that the saint lived in perpetual sanctity and at mass during the consecration went into ecstasy as though she were lifted off the ground that she didn't rest on any feet either her own or those of the chair and those present ran to take

turns passing their hands underneath with great con-
sternation at finding out it was so, and Agnese Bordin
has a mother who's curious and sat down next to the
deceased to see if she truly levitated herself from the
floor, because she was fat to boot, and she tried to pass
her hand under her shoes and the feet of the chair and
the hand passed under without hitting anything but air,
and the undersigned Dorotea Belan saw Agnese Bordin's mother pass her hand under the shoes of the
deceased and then under the chair and then back again
under the chair and then under the shoes and stand up
with her mouth wide open in total admiration, and the
undersigned Concetta noted many times that when the
priest raised the chalice, the deceased though remaining
seated leaned forward with her hands joined in the act
of prayer and immediately was lifted off the floor along
with the chair, Nota Bene: the levitation was by as much
as two fingers and a hand could pass under the shoes
and the chair of the deceased, and many people did so
pass their hands, the undersigned Casimira finding
herself one day at the saint's house saw her eating fish
from a plate when all of a sudden for some reason she
took the plate and threw it into the yard and wonder of
wonders the plate didn't break and the fish stayed on it,
by hearsay from the villagers she knows that when the
priest raised the chalice the saint would levitate and
there were many women and a few men who ran to pass
their hands under the chair and staring at each other
with astonishment said it was so, also the undersigned
Giuseppa Fin writes with her own hand and of her own

free will. that the deceased, the priest lifted the chalice and the deceased was lifted up too. and the priest lowered the chalice and the deceased too. to the greatest astonishment of everyone, who wanted to pass their hands under the chair to make certain, she's finished writing and please excuse the mistakes and recommend to the Lord one of his believers Giuseppa Fin, at this point the stranger had finished his wine and left the tavern while la Imbroja trotted along behind him to the door and to the cart and hurriedly turning the pages of her notebook she went over the lesson for him repeating by way of recapitulation the names of the signatories and when he left with his mule at a slow trot the woman raised her right hand and separating the index finger from the thumb by about two centimeters she smiled lording it over him because in his village so far as we know no one is capable of levitating by those two attested centimeters.

3. The race of Attila

To go and get married by bus is a great convenience and it's more of a luxury than cars because cars passing along walled-in roads can't be seen from the fields and so the wedding car remains half hidden while the bus is high and makes a great cloud of dust and its windows give off a huge glitter that tells the whole story to those working on both sides of the road with the result that there are always some of them who feel entitled to turn up at the feast, Narcisa would really have preferred cars because she didn't want to be too conspicuous but my brother was pleased with her and let her know it at supper by banging his big fist on the table which made the dishes rattle and caused her to spit the food out of her mouth and he said with a good-natured laugh bus the laugh of God Almighty must be more or less like that when after years of drought he decides then and there to open the sluice gates of heaven right onto the faithful drawn up in columns for the triduum and all of them scamper away disconcerted by the miracle except for the priest who takes shelter as slowly and majestically as a pharaoh besides everybody in the village has seen a few cars go by, once there was even a tourist who stopped one summer evening with his automobile on a green stretch along the road right next to a curve and there he put up a tent for himself and his wife who was very tall and well-dressed but with two green eyes like a crazy woman, the minute they heard about it the men in the tavern stopped playing cards and came by foot and bicycle to sit around the tent and spy out how the foreigners made love and then the German who was washing his face in a basin looked up with astonished eyes like the perfect kraut he was and barking he emptied the water from the basin on the nearest ones and then because the group was starting to become threatening he hastily folded the tent and departed in the direction of Montagnana, after all if he intends to sleep in our house without at least acknowledging our right to look at him it's better that he stay in his own house, unlike cars the bus doesn't go by except specifically for a wedding and it comes down for that purpose from Legnago in the province of Verona and whatever it may cost for such an important day it's still worth it, there's the problem that the bus always arrives late because the driver doesn't know the road and in fact that day too it arrived half an hour late when there were already a lot of people in the yard but for a day like this even the priest would close an eye, of course the bus could hold only a small number of the guests and the rest could follow by bicycle or stay and wait for the return wandering around the yard and in the fields but wihout visiting the cook who didn't want to be disturbed, so here's Narcisa departing in tears enthroned in full view in the front seat farther back sit my father smiling aimlessly and my mother who however hasn't opened her mouth for months and then all the others, in

53

front of the church they'll meet the bridegroom with his parents and Narcisa weeping will walk toward the priest who stands waiting on the first step of the altar with one eye more closed than usual and the other more wide open, even during catechism Don Panzetta has one eye closed and one open and his tongue sticks out sideways between his teeth when he moves around showing the children the illustrations in his book where you see the devil emerging from the flames hairy as an ape with horns and with his left hand holding a pitchfork with three prongs pointing downward each prong like an arrow with a triangular point that first goes into the flesh and then doesn't come out, more modern therefore than the pitchforks of us peasants which have clean smooth shining and increasingly pointed prongs thin as needles at the end and go in easily piercing the skin but they also come out easily and serve among other things to force the ox that's broken its chain to obey when an ox breaks its chain the woman who's left at home bolts the gate and rushes off by bicycle to the fields to tell her husband yelling all the way at the top of her lungs King's got loose or Giant, Spaniard's got loose or Paintbrush, Old Three Hundred's got loose, everybody in the village knows that Giant is harmless but rambunctious and when he doesn't get away it's simply because he's satisfied with the alfalfa you've given him real alfalfa and not wheat straw the Brusacasottis are so stingy that they often give their oxen yellow straw to eat and put special green glasses on them so they'll think it's green grass, everyone knows that Paintbrush gets his name from having a hide so smooth that it looks combed, everyone knows that Spaniard's horns itch and he's always scratching them against the wall and sometimes even against a person and my brother who knows this scratches him with his fingernails at the base of the horns and under the dewlaps every morning when he wakes up then the poor ox sticks out his neck so that my brother's finger can penetrate all the way between the everlasting folds and with dilated nostrils he enjoys the scratching and his smoky blue eyes seek out the smoky blue eyes of my brother and a soft and loving spirit flows back and forth between them because my brother knows very well what it is to have an itch, right after the war my father mother brother sister and I from having had to sleep in the barn while the arrogant Germans slept in our beds all caught scabies and we kept worrying the muscles of our armpits like horses tormented by flies and scratching our hands between one finger and another until they bled but without drawing the microbes out with the blood and getting rid of them finally we went to the doctor in Montagnana and he takes one look at my father's hand and gasps he puts on gloves looks at the hand again and gasps lets that hand drop and takes the other one and gasps and then jumping around like a cricket without a foot says get out of here get out and starts shoving my brother and me and then my father who however put up some resistance because he was trying to retrieve his cloak wait outside we wait outside with bowed heads until through the window he gives us the prescription and my father takes it to the pharmacist and the pharmacist makes him an ointment and because my father wants to take off his cloak he yells take it easy take it easy and my father pleased with such courtesy looks at us boys to reassure us and out of too much trust starts to sit down but the pharmacist who's been keeping an eye on him yells hey get up the ointment's ready that'll be so and so much my father pulls out his handful of coins tied up in a handkerchief and counts one two three the pharmacist loses patience and says that's enough he sends us away before we realize what's going on, every evening in the barn for weeks thereafter the men on one side and the women on the other we smeared ointment on our naked bodies to kill the scabies germs the ointment stung and attracted the flies that swarm in the barn lying on the straw I could never close my eyes also because of the sound of the ox chains for they didn't stop clanking for a moment and out of fear I used to stick my head in my father's big armpits and he'd console me and say I'm going to kill one of them but when that moment came before the Germans left he found one lone German and after years of waiting raised his ax to give him a great whack in the back between his neck and his ass but didn't have the courage to follow through, everybody knows how Old Three Hundred gets his name because that's his price and there's no bargaining about this price and there's not an ox worth that much all the way to Be Osso and Casale della Scodosia and every time my father as a joke spreads the word that Old Three Hundred is for sale middlemen come rushing on bicycles from all the nearby villages with ready offers in money and kind and proposals for various swaps and exchanges such as for example we give Old Three Hundred and the Macaco brothers will give us a cross-bred cow that produces more milk than piss and Bepi Macaco will hand over to us that triangular plot of land that borders our fields higher up and from which between November and April pools of water drain down and ruin our crops, but my father laughs in the face of this middleman who stands there measuring the ox's rump with a string and then with his face down and his eyes rolled up as though he were praying makes his crazy calculations to change centimeters into kilos and just to get his goat he goes up to him and asks Mantua? now you ought to know that around here to say to someone he's from Mantua is saying to him he's a thief, and to say to other people that one's from Mantua is like telling them not to let him get away, some years ago in fact a little group of Mantuan dealers went around the village with trucks and a local middleman who's since migrated God knows where and in the space of a day they visited all the families and bought all the wheat that was ready in sacks paying more for it than anyone could have asked and with the trick of the price they fooled us too, a few days later we heard that people from the Maio district had punctured the tires of the Mantuans' truck so that the carabinieri came on motorcycles, the carabinieri usually circulate on bicycles and they use motorcycles only for the more urgent cases, because the Maio people had previously weighed a sack on their own and it was so and so much and now when they weighed it again with the Mantuans give or take a little it weighed less and so they got suspicious and made them unload everything and started weighing all over again and two of the Maio men holding on their shoulders the beam on which the scale is hung noticed that one of the Mantuans is lame and that when he approaches the scale it oscillates and one side goes down, immediately they drop everything grab the lame man and drag him into the house and while the women run with pitchforks to puncture the tires of the truck so that it doesn't get away they take off the Mantuan's shoe and a-ha it turns out that in his shoe there's a magnet which jiggled the scale, his life was saved only by the carabinieri and from then on at the outskirts of the village when we sell wheat there's been a sign that says NO MANTUANS AL-LOWED even if the middleman isn't from Mantua my father still laughs in his face for as everybody knows my father hates crossbred cows because unlike purebreds they have great trouble giving birth, when a cow is about to calve the whole family has to be on the alert since this could be the night when help will be needed and of course the one who gets sent around at night on the bicycle without lights to ask for help is always me the relatives arrive like shadows toss their bicycles in the yard and jump into the stall where everything is ready rope salt grease and soap, with the grease and soap they smear the mother's natural cleft so that the calf can slide out easily without scraping and making her bleed, with the rope they tie the calf's legs as soon as it puts them

out and pull it toward life, as for the salt when everything is over and the men have sat down a woman
scatters it by the handful all over the skin of the little calf
who is much surprised by what it sees and totters in the
cold on its four legs which are spread so wide that they
don't seem to grow under the belly but at the four sides,
the salt is indispensable because when the cow has
finished emptying her belly she collects herself a little
and loves her little one licking it over and over with her
raspy tongue to the point where she might do it harm by
removing its damp coat, here's where the salt fixes
everything and the cow stops licking but with her
tongue out turning her head to the woman she moos
plaintively as though to ask why did you put salt all over
it, everybody knows that King was castrated badly and
his balls weren't completely cut off and so he's half bull
and half ox or rather he's still an ox but some days he's
a bull and then he gets on his feet strains his legs pulls
with his neck crack goes the chain and in the stall with
its bolted doors such hell breaks loose that by now the
other oxen have understood that King is a little out of
the ordinary since those who are castrated think it's the
normal thing to be, therefore when the woman arrives
in the fields yelling that this one or that one has got
loose the men rush home and there they find half the
village already gathered to enjoy the spectacle and
doing nothing to help, then it's a matter of trapping the
ox in an ever narrower space and from there driving
him huffing and puffing toward the stall poking him
with those pitchforks that go quite easily in and out

through the skin making a little drop of blood spurt, the devil on the other hand uses a less crude pitchfork with a straight handle and more painful prongs and it must be awful to find oneself dead afterwards in his yard hounded like an ox that doesn't want to enter the stall of Hell, during catechism lessons the priest showed us the pictures in his little book and pointed with his finger to the hellish billygoat all teeth and while we looked enraptured at the devil in person the priest observed us gloomily with one eye half closed and one wide open and his tongue sticking out sideways between his lips, just the way he's now observing Narcisa who enters through the women's door and slowly slowly all too slowly approaches the altar with lowered eyes and kneels down on the cushions in front of the balustrade, as in every marriage the church is so full of people that there's no room for the children, so I wait outside and when everything is over the first I see to emerge is Panzetta who on being invited to the banquet by my brother keeps saying no no and walking quickly to the bus takes the seat next to the driver who feeling himself honored now takes his hat off to drive, when we arrive home with the bus packed full we find many more people in the yard than when we had left but the system works all the same because if by chance the cook has miscalculated and we run short of meat we can be sure that as soon as he notices there's not enough the poultry man will arrive with a full coop and the whole bunch can be bought killed and prepared in a great hurry, the feasting begins in the open under the vine arbors where my brother has set out the tables joined one to another as for the Last Supper, the tables aren't all the same height and together they look like a roller coaster with people shouting every so often hurray for the newly-weds and then the cook gets annoyed and makes an appearance and so they yell hurray for the cook, after four or five minutes men start going back and forth between the tables and the trees because the new wine doesn't stay for long in the body and instinct and tradition lead them to urinate against trees both because in this way they're half hidden and decency is observed and also so that the liquid which is a fertilizer doesn't get wasted, if you gaze all around the fields you see one next to another a tree and a man a tree and a man a tree and a man looking like all those hanged men the morning after the bridges were blown up and the Germans had roused out of their homes some thirty men who knew nothing about it and loaded them on a truck with hands and feet tied and the noose around their necks and as the truck started moving a fascist took the free end of the rope and threw it up and over a branch and so the luckless man tied to that rope felt himself being jerked up and out of the truck and bang he was hanged, when the truck had gone all that was left was a row of trees each with a man who had been smashed against it and already Jija was there groping from one body to another in search of Jijo while a German ran after her barking, the Germans when they get mad are unable to speak in words and try as they may they must bark first because they descend from

61

Attila, Attila's mother was kept locked up by her father the king because it was known that she would have a son so warlike that history would remember only him, the mother however got bored at always being alone and so she asked her father if she could at least have the company of a dog and her father granted her wish by sending into her bedroom a restless guard dog with big fangs thinking that this way his daughter would be even more thoroughly and insuperably isolated, but the daughter began to play with the dog and take him into her bed and she liked the way his body constantly quivered and his gaze that was always intent on his own business and in short she had a son by him who was named Attila, this son was all man except for his nails and eyes which were those of a dog, and he reasoned like a man but when all of a sudden he lost his temper in order to clear a path for his words he first had to vomit his rage by barking three times, and it's precisely from him that the Germans descend because before coming out with something almost like words they always have to bark RAUS RAUS RAUS, if then by chance gazing out over the fields you see a tree unpaired with a man you're immediately overcome by the need to urinate and before you know it you can't resist the beguiling wish to get up unbutton your pants and hurry to occupy that empty spot before anyone else gets there, by now under every tree a conspicuous puddle has already formed and some can't go without urinating for more than ten minutes so they take their table and move it for convenience closer to the chosen tree which means that by now the banquet is no longer unified but broken up into small tables and at the farthest one seated all alone and eating in slow and infinitely sad mouthfuls as if he were suffering the punishments of hell is Berto Oco, who came home a year ago on a Red Cross van to be dropped off with his bundle in the midst of his family who didn't recognize him and therefore couldn't decide whether to give him anything to eat and even now when he eats a little too much they have strong doubts about his identity besides he really does have a screw loose, once they took him to Montagnana with the cart and when they stopped at the train crossing he started to get excited his lower lip and left eye trembling as if they were about to depart from his body, furthermore this eye was always half closed like a window left ajar in the room of a sick man, and when the train streaked by it was as though he'd had a wrenching shock throughout his body and panting heavily he catapulted out of the cart and ran across fields and ditches like a horse pursued by flies, another fear burst out of him even in the very first days and that was to be called by name in a loud voice by several persons at once, then his eye closed on him completely like a locked window in a house in mourning, his human figure looked like a target silhouette on which someone had drawn a bead, he would stop in his tracks without turning around his legs spread and his knees a little flexed as though he were doing something in his pants and slowly raise his hands in a sign of surrender, when the boys from the Mill district discovered these fits they got a charge out of

63

waiting for him five or six of them at a time in front of
his house and then shouting his name in chorus and
when he froze at the corner like a scarecrow they
pretended to shoot him RAT TAT TAT, now the wine
has filled them up stomach belly bladder and veins, no
matter how often they go to urinate they're no longer
able to discharge it the level is so high that some begin
to spew it out of their mouths, the important thing now
is to be able to tell the different kinds of drunkenness
because there's the crying jag and the talking jag which
are no danger to others, but there's also such a thing as
going on a rampage and those who do use a stick and
there's also such a thing as seeing cockroaches and
those who do use a knife and the reason it's called that
is because the drunkard for example right now Bepi the
Friar suddenly leaps up among the dishes on the table
because he's seen a string of cockroaches go by on the
ground when there really aren't any there this kind of
drunkenness dilates the pupils like those of an ox and
makes the heart rattle inside the chest cavity like a rag
flapping in the wind, at this point anyone who's still
lucid may notice among the trees or behind the corners
of the house children watching with frightened eyes
trying to distinguish exactly what kind of drunkenness
each one's father is showing so they can report to their
mothers who have sent them to find out whether
they're in for a light-hearted thrashing, since then you
can even sleep in your own bed with your husband who
after beating you up calms down and lets you take the
stick away from him without protesting too much, or if

he's intent on some darker business with a knife, in which case it would be a good idea to take refuge in the hayloft or barn or out in the open though not even there can a woman feel safe except for the wife of Bepi the Friar who can calmly take shelter in the stable and stretch out against the belly of one of the oxen fully aware that her husband hasn't enough courage to come in the stable even by day ever since that horrible thing happened which I'll tell you about in a moment.

4. *The double history of the Dog Man*

The whole history concerning my village has the essential character of being outside time not in the sense that reality becomes fable but in the opposite sense that fable also becomes reality, meaning that everything that's happened in stories is destined to happen at any time and on this basis the old people could tell us that the Germans were such and so and that in time we'd find out for ourselves, as though each generation must unfailingly have its own experience with war and the Germans, and as far as I'm concerned this conception has been perfectly true, as a result the peasant doesn't know whether Attila passed through these parts twenty-five years ago or twenty thousand or whether he's still to come and indeed he's convinced that even to bring up such a problem is a waste of time because the chief problem is to know what Attila does and what one ought to do when he passes through bear it in mind and teach it in exact terms to one's children, now I myself don't know if all the events that entered into my memory during the time of my childhood actually happened then or had happened thousands of years before or after, but I realize that the only way to explain them is not to leave their occurrence that is to say their truth out of consideration because the fact is that for us history becomes a parable just as Sunday parables are

history. The new house where the Maroèli family lives,
but you can't even say they live there because actually
they're never inside and the house is always empty so
that ever since the door rotted away in the rain and cold
and crumbled to bits no one has seen fit to repair it and
now the wind goes in and out as it likes scattering the
spores of mold on all the walls, it's called the house of
the Dog Man not because the men who lived there are
called dogs but because when they were digging the
hole for the foundations after the first shovelfuls of dirt
they found a skeleton with teeth set in a snarl a German
helmet on its head and a dog chain around its neck,
since the Maroèli house is isolated in the middle of the
countryside almost outside our village and only the fogs
visit it every day, the Maroèlis themselves show up once
a year in our tavern and once in the Scodosia tavern,
and that's why there are two stories going around about
that skeleton, one told in Scodosia and the other in our
village, and of course it's not that one is true and one
false but both are true like two parables and each
parable holds for the village destined to understand it,
the people in Scodosia say that this German was left
behind during the retreat and having lost his bearings
wandered through the fields barking at the moon and
the peasants got together and formed a posse to hunt
him down getting closer to his cry every night and one
night when the peasants too had almost got lost and
were sitting in a ditch to sleep on their cloaks all of a
sudden the clouds broke and a full moon came out,
immediately the German began to bay there close by

almost in their ears long howls that struck horror to the countryside, so the men jumped up and formed a circle around him and penned him in while he leaped back and forth trying to get out and then they grabbed him by the back of his neck and lifted him up from the ground howling like the siren of the sugar refinery in Montagnana and with a dog chain they tied him by the neck to the largest plane tree and went home satisfied to their wives, the howls of the dog man swelled to the size of a mountain all that first night, the next night they sank to a hill, and on the third night they flattened out completely like a plain without crickets, and then the men returned with their spades and found him silent but with his eyes wide open so that even when they poked him with sticks they couldn't really be sure that he was dead in any case there was no point thinking about it and they detached the chain from the tree whose bark was all worn away by the circling of the dog, who had also worn all the hair off his neck, and there they buried him with the chain tied and there the skeleton still is and its ghost wanders around and if by chance someone who knows the story sits down on a log to eat a piece of bread, in a twinkling the Ghost Dog trots up to him filches the hunk of bread from his hand and eats it crouching on the ground, people in our village when they say Dog Man don't mean the German but are referring instead to Bepi the Friar who like a dog had bitten a German's nose in the interval between the flight of the fascists and the arrival of the Americans, that interval lasted a whole night which so far is the most tragic night experienced by the village during my generation which is not to say that it won't soon be repeated more or less the same way or even worse because now a new generation is coming up and it's inevitable that it too will have its experiences, just exactly who the German of our parable was at the beginning nobody knows for sure and anyway no one considers it important, maybe it was the one who arrogantly entered our yard with a squad of soldiers went up into the hayloft calculated with a glance how much feed there was decided how much to take and how much to leave behind barked to his men who immediately set to work moving their necks eyes elbows and knees oddly like marionettes, he came in the house to pay my father who was waiting for him hopelessly and vengefully sitting in the big armchair with sleeves rolled up arms folded and eyes staring and here he started sniffing the smell of coffee that my mother was serving us and all of a sudden he turned nice and polite paid us what we asked with money that a week later became worthless paper and cordially begged signore signora you got a little coffee? and from that day on he passed through the village every morning at an early hour going in this or that house to have a drop of coffee as pleasant and talkative as the wolf of Gubbio after the miracle and he made friends with the children of the district who touched his big leather belt his high boots the barrel of his automatic pistol the wooden handle of his hand grenade, or maybe it was the German who on a sultry empty summer afternoon with the sun beating down arrived in a jeep so silent that no one heard it coming drove closely around our house like an arrow hitting a gust of wind athwart and entered the yard where the old women dressed in black were sitting with their backsides on the ground, jumped down without a sound took a few long strides stopped in the middle of the threshing floor with his boots spread wide and the visor of his cap pulled low over his eyes with his head bent and one hand holding the cigarette between his lips it seemed to the old women that he was thinking and nothing else actually out of the corner of his eye he was taking in the entire perimeter of the yard with scrupulous attention and with his ear he was sifting even the faintest sounds and when a hen went cluck he threw away his cigarette butt bounded three steps to the left uncovered the coop dragged it into the middle of the yard and took out the hens one by one to kill them he held them by the head and whirled them around their wings flapping until the neck snapped and the body fell to the ground and the head remained in his hand with the beak drooling and the tongue twisted, then the soldiers collected the decapitated hens one by one filling the jeep while the German tossed the heads at the feet of the old women whose scowling faces shrank tight as a fist as they divided up these bloody remains, but at the end a miracle occurred and before his departure standing upright like a kind god on the jeep between the attendant angels seated at his feet the German spoke a few words and at the feet of the starving women a few hens rained down as though from heaven, or maybe it was the German who when the Bissi house was burned down with the whole Bissi family locked inside had been set to guard the door facing the river and when the door collapsed in the flames and through the opening young Bissi fled naked with his hair on fire and jumped in the river, he held his fire while his comrades didn't even spare the mother who had been the first to awaken and jump down from the window, anyway the fact is that in the last month the rumor spread that one German had turned good and thrown in his lot with the partisans acting as a spy against his comrades, and on the night that the bridge was to be blown up he was sent ahead to distract the sentinels by talking to them until the signal came, and afterwards he remained hidden in the ditches in the open countryside revealing himself only to the peasants who worked far from their houses in order to get a few bowls of wine from them and in the last nights getting in the habit of sleeping in Bepi the Friar's stable though everybody knew that Bepi the Friar had a personal score to settle with the Germans ever since the time Quisanò was ambushed, once Quisanò came to our village too to play the bully and went around with a coiled rope on his shoulder ready to hang someone and going from house to house he told the Germans how many men there were in each family and the women immediately had to explain where their husbands and sons were or else the house was set on fire, the men hiding out in the woods or fields found out about it and gathered in a group and at dawn went to the crossroads to prepare an ambush and they stretched a steel wire across the road so strong that motorcycles and jeeps wouldn't break it and they themselves hid alongside the road under the bushes in the ditch with knives in their hands and along comes the jeep taking the curve smoothly and without skidding escorted by four motorcycles with machine guns slung on their backs and Quisanò is last with the rope on his shoulder in front of him the Germans sit smoking and don't even offer him a cigarette, the steel wire is like the sword of the archangel Gabriel its blade forever extended to bring equal ruin on those who sin directly or by proxy, the motorcyclists are the first to be grabbed by the throat from their handlebars and flipped over on their backs, then the driver of the jeep and the Germans who now on their feet are picked up by their boots and sent sprawling on their noses in the dust while the car turns over in the ditch and bursts into flames, some of them emerge from the smoking ruin and stand up but our villagers are already waiting on the road and plant their knives under the right ear and slowly make a deep cut in the watermelon passing under the chin to the left ear with the same satisfaction as the hog butchers bending over a pig, except for Quisanò who gets taken obligingly by the arms and escorted twenty yards away and hanged to a fig tree with his own rope, the news spreads in a flash and arrives at our house when the Germans are already fanning out through the countryside organizing a dragnet burning the fields of dry wheat and combing the green meadows inch by inch, women with children dash through the culverts without even know-

ing where they're going while men fleeing barefoot
sharpen their wild instincts and dig themselves hide-
aways under the roots of trees or lairs in the marshes
settling their heads bellies backsides and legs in perfect
mimicry the way hares do, loving the signs of animal life
like the frog that puffs out its throat and restrains its
croaking or the cricket that puts its head out of its hole
and climbs up the swaying blade of grass with motionless antennae to observe the horizon or the blackbird
that hops from one dry twig to another and doesn't spin
around frightened in the air because by now even the
birds and beasts have learned to alter their behavior
depending on whether a German or a peasant goes by,
it was the dawn of a summer night so humid that it
seemed to be drizzling but actually the water wasn't
coming down in drops but was condensed in mid-air so
you had only to stand outside for a quarter of an hour
and you felt your clothes as soaked and heavy as though
you had waded across the river and your eyelids dripping like a leaking faucet, the wheat fields at that hour
had trouble sustaining a series of small fires that strug-
gled to unite in a single fire and flared up here and there
irregular as short circuits and over the countryside the
smoke from the fires unrolled in low waves punctuated
by the long and occasional tolling of the bells which
made it difficult to lay bare the earth's skeleton in order
to survey it and pinpoint the hidden fugitives indeed in
that ragged cloud bank they were more secure than
before and could shift from one place to another following the more overgrown trails to escape the Germans

who were advancing wheezing and coughing in a line and find a better hiding place in a deeper hole or between bigger roots or in denser underbrush or in a patch of grass surrounded by more water, in the end each group of Germans was supplied with a dog since the dragnet was not having great results and already our village seemed to be without a living soul, the dog was held on the leash by the German at the center of each line and in this manner the squads advanced with their weapons leveled along the plowed furrows hardly glancing at the areas denuded by the fire lingering instead in the areas that were still grassy, the dog had never been trained for exercises of this kind and its sense of smell was confused by the fire and smoke and the earth bewildered it with the thousands of violent odors it emitted and the forms of life it restored to the light crickets that to their own surprise jumped three yards water snakes that darted like lightning bolts and disappeared vertically into the first hole wild cats that sprang with tails erect for hundreds of yards so swiftly that in seeing the grass sway at their passage you couldn't tell where they'd started or where they'd arrived whole families of rats skipping about like tiny apes upright on their hind legs sluggish frogs that listened stupidly as their backs went from soaking wet to moist dry to burning dry and then burst in so many swollen blisters insects and eyeless moths living in holes without air and without light white of skin and without motion born for a the single slow and unconscious function of reproduction to die immediately thereafter

large ants floating on the water or dew and flammable
bursting with the egg-bombs in their bellies igniting the
water like gasoline grasshoppers that traversed the
smoke only to burn up twenty yards farther on and fall
in the form of tepid pulp porcupines curled up and
hiding within themselves like coals under the ashes, the
German shepherd sniffed everything with its nose constantly to the ground and breathed and puffed charcoal
ashes in small black heavy clouds that tarred its lungs,
the squad at the end of a level stretch ran into the other
squad coming in the opposite direction and they paused
standing erect and fearful as devils amid the flames of
Hell holding a powwow in the same language as their
dogs who also greeted each other and muzzle to muzzle
mutually exchanged the ashes in their lungs, it happened right there in our fields known as the Lowlands
where Bepi the Friar who had been the ringleader of the
ambush against Quisanò had hidden himself and he still
had the knife in his hand and so as not to die by surprise
he had settled himself on his back face up in a mud
puddle in the midst of the wheat the German with the
dog came right up this very furrow and Bepi the Friar
who had heard the insects pass distinctly by species and
had felt the fire when the water under his backside and
loins and neck had become warmish now heard the dog
come snarling and pulling on the leash right toward him
but much as he tried to turn his eyes without moving his
head he was unable to see it and while he was trying to
calculate the distance of the sound of its breathing he
felt a great wave of damp hot breath on his head and as

he rolled his eyes backwards the dog's long fangs grazed his forehead and through the opening between its front teeth came its breath and its fleeting tongue, for a split second it was as though he couldn't think and immediately afterwards he guessed that that moment of non-thought had been the passage from the here and now to the hereafter and indeed he remembered that through his whole body starting at the point on his forehead licked by the dog a thick shudder had run all the way to his knees and to his shoes and after the shudder his body was colder and the water warmer as though he had unwittingly pissed in it in fact his belly and thighs were warm while all the rest was cold or rather not cold it just wasn't there any more and this was the second time it wasn't there because a moment before when a man had looked at him over a dog with the eyes of a dog as if the dog had four eyes as if the dog were also a man as if the man were also a dog he had tried to move his arm but his arm no longer had the knife or rather the arm no longer had the body and by itself without the body it was unable to lift itself it was as though the dog by grazing his forehead with its teeth had made his thought recede into his belly which became warm and as though for a moment the man had wanted his head to be the head of another, the man stayed this way for whole days succeeding in thinking only at disconnected intervals, little by little as his thought disappeared as though the lights were being extinguished all over the world he felt a great inertia and when he re-emerged from the darkness of the uncon-

scious he tried disgustedly and when he re-emerged
from the darkness of the unconscious he tried disgustedly to keep himself from thinking, his thought more-
over was shapeless and without memories and
fragmentary as though with each flicker of consciousness he was reborn differently until after all these births
once by chance he was reborn as himself and immediately he sent his thought to the right side of his body
and his right hand moved, immediately he withdrew his
thought for fear that it was too soon and decided to bide
his time in order to have less fear, the thing that
frightened him most was not the lack of a future because
this is something we're used to it was the lack of a past
not a painful sensation but a stupefying one which to
the spirit is like the absence of weight is to the body, not
having a memory was exactly like not having weight
and indeed he was weightless as though floating on the
world and his right arm was not attached but stuck to
his body like a leaf held next to the tree trunk by the
current, to raise it weightless as it was made no sense
since it would also have been able to remain suspended
in mid-air, better to wait for it to weigh slowly on the
ground so as to be able to wrench it back and again have
it definitely as his own, not having memory was exactly
like not having identity and thus not even importance
and if someone at that moment had killed him he would
not have defended himself because it wasn't worth the
trouble and this idea of being killed was the first one
that came to him like the most natural sensation in the
world and once it had entered into his brain it found it

completely empty and so there it stayed for a long time,
but instead of becoming a long time in the future it
became long in the past turning slowly from sensation
into memory so that instead of thinking that someone at
that moment might kill him the man realized that he
was thinking that someone at that moment might *kill
him again* while lying there without suffering but immediately afterwards he realized that he was *thinking again*
that someone might kill him and thereupon he began to
suffer and he thought hard toward the right with an
effort lifting his heavy right hand toward the right side
of his forehead to feel it without pressing his hand
which stuck there by its own swollen and sluggish
weight, during this gesture some other part of his body
had moved (as though his body were whole [bodies are
whole]) and in moving had felt a coldness less cold on
the body that is to say a damp warmth (meaning water)
and for a while he went on suffering without thinking
but deliberately keeping the notion of weight narrow
not wanting to lose it though confusedly aware that it
was precisely the sense of weight that brought with it
the pain so that it was as though the pain were a burden
too or rather it was a burden precisely because his head
had become very heavy and the man tried to discover
that is to say remember from which side one sent the
thought to raise one's head and since the thought had
already passed through the right side he tried to make it
pass again but instead of raising his hand from his
forehead he only succeeded in pulling it away until it fell
alongside him and as it fell he again felt that less cold

coldness that is to say that warmth that warm water and then he remembered having felt that warm water with a part of his body that was not the hand but try as he might he was unable to understand that is remember on what side that part of the body was and what it looked like and whether it had felt the cold by itself or by sending it to the head, the same thought of not being able to raise his hand had pulled it back and now being unable to raise his head he let it drop to the right so half of his head and thereby half his mouth and one eye went under water with the feeling of a coldness less cold that is of warmth and immediately the man understood that is remembered that the first part that had felt warm was neither the head nor the hand but another part that was like the center of the body and so meanwhile he tried to send his thought first to that center then to the hand then to that center and to the hand thus succeeding in reconstituting a great part of his unity and this operation was so important and fundamental that the man by engaging in it to the point of suffering thereby prevented himself from listening to another part of his body that was there and was resuming its existence namely the left ear which now found itself out of the water and open to the sky and though there was no sound over the world nevertheless he heard the absence of sounds namely silence while up until now under water he had not heard anything not even the silence and this matter of the left ear was something very important because now his thought could also arrive on the left indeed it paused more willingly on the left because the left eye could see better than the right indeed the right eye was as though closed or rather as though full while the left eye floated on the water and was looking at the water until by shifting itself further it also saw some blades of grass upright over the water and for a timeless period it remained motionless staring at them because there was something to be understood in them and in fact at the end of that moment the idea took shape that these were red blades of grass over green water and the red was an unexpected surprise but then the idea dissolved and when it again took shape it was another idea namely that these were green blades of grass over red water and the red surprised and alarmed him and alarm being more agile than thought it invaded his whole body from right to left from head to foot like a little animal that slips easily into a narrow tunnel examining its twists and turns in search perhaps of an opening of light and not finding it returns to its point of departure that is to the head where from alarm it turned back into thought, by now the unity of the body had been gained and the man felt himself to be something longer and heavier so that he seemed to be sinking lower while the sky was receding and in the effort not to sink and to keep things from receding he clung to the world with his hands and with his feet and with his gaze, now farther away he could see the scattered motionless trees on the plain and through their branches filtered a drenched and solid light as though it were not yet day or as though it were day no longer the sun was nowhere to be seen and it was impossible to guess on what side it would rise or if it was dead and would never rise or set again but the overcast sky between him and the sun gave off on the world a clear uniform haze that chilled, now he was cold because the water in which he lay was less warm that is to say colder than his reconstituted body and as he slowly felt the water becoming cold that is his body becoming warm he felt the weight dissolve and become pain, first a dull and widespread pain in the form of a fear of consciousness that is of fearful consciousness, then in the form of a feeling of impotence bordering on horror, then in the form of solitude as though he feared to find himself the only living being in the unknown world, now he felt that to raise his head he needed to be able to make that particular movement and pushing with his hands he slowly raised his head but his head constantly fell back and therefore he had to raise it repeatedly, it was as though he were a dead man who keeps going up and down on the waves and doesn't know what forces are keeping him afloat, in the end he realized that the world was bobbing and rotating around him just as though the world itself were floating on the water and then looking at himself he understood that he was on his knees and turning around he saw impressed in the gurgling reddish mud the shape of the human figure with its arms outspread and thus kneeling and contorted at the feet of the disordered world he seemed like Adam at the moment of creation.

Our whole village knows this story but like all country

villages believes that no knowledge exists unless it's complete and therefore doesn't like to have empty spaces either at the beginning or the end or in the middle and it fills these empty spaces with forms and characters and parables that slowly over the centuries become specific until they acquire a definitive and concrete consistency higher than the other facts of history, and for example the fact that after Biscazzo's death a roll of paper was heard bouncing down the stairs as though Biscazzo dead and transformed into paper had been in a twinkling rolled into Hell to burn up instantly is a fact more precise in its characteristics and emotions and more capable of being transmitted from father to son than more direct and personal experiences many details of which always escape us as does sometimes even the occurrence itself, all the things that Bepi the Friar talked about as soon as he was back in circulation diminished to a role of secondary importance while the mystery that excited people's imaginations was that split second between the appearance and disappearance of the Germans with the dog, the one who thought about it more than anyone else was of course Bepi the Friar and when after several days he had finished thinking about it the story came out complete and perfect, ready to be packaged and sealed and reopened by each generation of posterity, he had tried to turn his eyes without moving his head but had not been able to see it and while he was trying to calculate the distance of the sound of its breathing he felt a great wave of damp hot breath on his face and when he rolled his eyes backwards, like this, the dog's long fangs grazed his forehead and through the opening between its teeth came its breath and its fleeting tongue, for a split second it was as though everything had stopped in fact the line of Germans had halted seeing the dog pause and behind the dog the face of the German holding it on the leash loomed high against the sky and the buried man looked at the standing man who was looking at him but at that moment a lark which the fire fitfully scorching the marsh had reached and driven out of its nest flew up from the ground right next to him and stayed at a height of three or four feet flapping its wings until the German with the dog caught it by slowly stretching out his hand and he showed it to his comrades using a new language that made it seem that he was laughing and the others laughed so much that they seemed to be responding in the same new language until the man lying on the ground thought they were in a cheerful mood and so he got to his knees to look around and saw that they were staring at him in a long line with laughing mouths but dogs' eyes while the German with the dog put the lark on his shoulder and some of those around him took aim, at the last moment the lark sprang upward into the infinite and he plunged down headlong, during the retreat Bepi the Friar planted himself at his gate to watch the Germans go by, first the tanks making a sound of branches sweeping the earth to cleanse the world of good feelings then a jeep or two with a sleeping man driving and a sleeping man on watch and all the other sleepers sleeping, then ragged and disordered groups on foot preceded by one in torn pants some thirty yards ahead showing them his ass like a beacon, then nothing more and then again a lone straggler perched on a bicycle like a tourist and finally one on horseback with the eyes of a dragon who came along tormenting his exhausted horse with a pitchfork and dismounted right in front of Bepi the Friar saying water he went in the house saying water to take some bread saying water that his horse refused to eat and hastily he mounted the horse who moved off slowly and before disappearing he turned around saying with a frightened look water, anyway the Americans by now were at the Adige and the Germans arriving at the river and no longer finding the bridge drove their truck into the water thinking it would float at least a little but it sank immediately to the bottom right next to the bank, a few Germans desperate to get across went into houses and took barrels for themselves which they opened at one end and dropped in the river and then jumped inside convinced that the current would carry them out to the middle and then over to the other side instead the Adige dragged them chattering and staring and longing for the river bank all the way from Legnago to Chioggia to dump them in the Adriatic like dead chickens, it would really seem as though just when they were on the point of dying these warriors turned fishermen wanted to waste time on a gigantic hunting and fishing expedition, during that whole clear balmy windless day the river with its half-sunken barrels acted as a great cableway from life to death because at Chioggia the fishermen

who had become warriors awaited them in their own
barrels planted solidly behind the islets and they waited
for the German carried into the sea to begin his great
maneuvers to take advantage of the waves and get
himself thrown up on the shore and with a single shot
they pierced the barrel just a hair beneath the waterline
and cocking their ears they heard the German caught
between air and water invent a new language because
barking no longer did any good, by now it was night
and Bepi the Friar ran to call One-Arm who understands
these things and little Bissi who had escaped the mas-
sacre of his family, and together they eavesdropped at
the door of the stable trying to distinguish the breathing
of the oxen from that of the man and hear whether the
man was asleep or awake, he was sleeping face up in the
straw his mouth open and emitting such a breath of
wine you'd think he was in the tavern and Bepi the Friar
was the first to look at him the lantern in his hand
bending over an inch from his nose, then he handed the
lantern to One-Arm who stood there gazing for a while,
then to little Bissi who no sooner did he have the lantern
than he dashed without speaking to the door and
stopped, the oxen were sleeping and ruminating lying
comfortably in their black dung on their big bellies so
overswollen that if you'd stuck a pin in their flanks they
might have exploded, when little Bissi without looking
raised the lantern to illuminate the scene Bepi the Friar
and One-Arm removed the bars from the bolted doors
and a sharp sound of metal was heard the oxen were
frightened and got to their feet their chains clanking in

85

unison and the German woke up rolling his eyes and just in time to see three hands rushing to grab him because at that very moment little Bissi threw down the lantern and yelling at the top of his lungs clambered up a beam, it was only One-Arm who hit him because the Friar stood for a moment as though paralyzed by the cries and stayed there writhing with the bar in his hands, but the fight had begun with the German who was no longer there and they had to find him in the darkness among the maddened animals who also were trying to gore each other, while One-Arm and the Friar cautiously felt the bellies of the oxen little Bissi's lament came from the rafters like a whine, stretching out a hand they felt cloth not hair which once more unleashed the struggle with the German who leaped over an ox in a single bound from high above the chaos came the loud cries of little Bissi as though he were the one they were killing, it was those cries in particular that drove One-Arm and the Friar to such fury that when all of a sudden it became very light and the German already half dead stood up on his feet still without understanding anything the two of them threw themselves on him with the iron bars yelling to drown out that other yelling that instead hung over the whole scene and the German died without hearing his own voice or knowing what he himself was saying, the lantern had set the straw on fire and now everything could be seen clearly the frightened animals strained their necks to break their chains little Bissi had fallen from the rafters but had rushed immediately to the bolted door and pressing against it with his whole body and teeth he pounded with his open hands wailing loudly and his whole body jerking back and forth as in an act of coitus, and the German lying on the floor seemed to be making an effort to get up again, calmly the two men stamped on the flames to extinguish them then hung the relighted lantern and opened the door whereupon little Bissi immediately calmed down gazing around as though he were looking for something and in the end turning around he saw the corpse and he looked at it for several minutes gasping and sniveling but with not much wailing until he realized that they were silently handing him the lantern and so he took it and without looking at the scene keeping his eyes to the ground or to one side he escorted the two others who transported the corpse far into the open countryside, there they set it down because first it was necessary to dig the hole the shovel was ready and while the Friar dug as fast as he could One-Arm kept watch on little Bissi from behind to make sure he didn't run away the Friar was also getting more and more excited and when finally the hole seemed deep enough to him he threw the shovel aside moaning, One-Arm noted with a shiver that it was a moan quite similar to little Bissi's, the Friar threw himself on the dead man's head as though he wanted to embrace him and dragged him into the hole while One-Arm pushed from behind as best he could and while with their hands and feet they both covered him with dirt little Bissi calmed down and sobbing softly turned to look at the poorly lit scene in time to see the most horrible thing, the head was just barely covered with a thin layer of earth and the first dog that went by could have unearthed the dead man's face with a single stroke of its paw, the nose actually stuck out like a summons it was there like an invitation and on that invitation the Friar moaning struck a blow with the shovel cutting it at the base then he flung himself forward to rip it away with either his hands or teeth but the minute little Bissi started whimpering he pulled him down and rolled on top of him to shut him up and so they fought biting each other and moaning while on the distant roads the last Germans passed in silence amid the explosions of stray bombs and the shots of a few tardy suicides and these are the reasons why Bepi the Friar came to be called by us the Dog Man and since our village has no boundaries marked on the terrain, which means that the mail for the farthest houses can be brought either by the postman for our village who comes on Monday and Friday or the postman for the neighboring villages who comes three times a week, all of us have ever since considered Bepi the Friar to be from another village as though the boundaries of our own began just on this side where misfortunes begin, the insane, the paralytics, the homeless, the sufferers from sleeping sickness and loss of memory, the crippled, the starving, but all belonging to the race of men and not crossed with dogs like the Germans.

5. *Perfect likenesses*

Our recollection of even the most serious events that happen in our lives always begins at the edges, from some bizarre detail outside the center, as though recollections were suspended sideways in our memory, or as though it were our habit to enter the area they enclose by an oblique and secret path: of the death of the Fisherman, who was always alone and slept in the canebrakes and never cut his beard because it was useful to him for drying his hands so that now he looked more like an ape than ever and seeing his form from afar it was hard to imagine that this was a human figure, I remember especially that they had to collect him piece by piece to reassemble him in a kneading trough and thus transport him home as though on a stretcher and from there my memory becomes more precise and turning back a little I see the Fisherman put his foot in the water and burst into fragments in the sky amid a spray of drops that never stopped falling and simultaneously, shaken by the blast, the children from the area flew from all sides to collect the bones and put them back together but here the problems began because for the first time we realized with astonishment that the banks of the river were full of bones the bones of drowned cows dogs geese making it necessary to set up a committee of experts then and there partly by election partly by self-appointment to make a careful examination of the bones recovered before pronouncing that they belonged to the dead man, but even with this institution copied from civilization no one could have all the necessary guarantees and in short the Fisherman's poor children remained for a long while faced with an embarrassing choice between two piles of bones, those approved and those discarded, before carting them away in the kneading trough; and of the death of the little Rapacina boy I remember there was a fly crawling on his nose and around the perimeter of his open mouth and that the mother didn't want to shut him in the coffin with the fly because suppose it would eat him alive and that on the other hand she couldn't kill it with the fly swatter without doing harm to her son and so she kept blowing and blowing on the fly so hard she almost tore away its wings but it stood firm in the middle of the wind its feet well planted in the flesh until the father got annoyed and with a swat and an oath crushed it with a long red sash which the mother with a whimper rushed to clean by wetting it with saliva, all this without the little corpse even being aware of it and this for me who witnessed it as a child was the first and clearest demonstration of what it means to be dead forever; and of Patrizia's arrival in our house, which has been by far the most important event in my life to date, I remember in particular having to give up my afternoon snack but at this point I see that I'm getting awfully far ahead of the story. That morning Panzetta was going around the village with a pencil and a notebook with cross-ruled paper in his hand and he showed up early at our house and this was a very great honor for us who had no longer deserved it ever since the year before, that is a few months after my sister's wedding, when Panzetta had rushed in frantically with his mouth twisted and didn't even bother to respond to the invitation to eat with us as he had done so often, on these occasions I was always the one left without soup, but without wasting time had immediately declared that if that's how things were there had been no need to pull the leg of God Almighty but to have been satisfied to have the wedding take place in the afternoon and not in the morning, and without ringing the bells and without putting the carpets in the church and without requiring a sung mass, since our Eve had already done some singing on her own with her fiancé and had even it would seem sung the song to the end, and the fiancé had responded with the refrain and everything, at this point Panzetta turned on his heel and went out his soutane flapping like the wind while my father and mother blushing with shame and unable to speak sat staring at the soup and my brother in addition to the trembling of his jaws rolled his eyes as though he were about to have a stroke, then without saying a word they separated my father going to the fields my mother upstairs and my brother to the barn, I stayed there coolly gulping down the food I was entitled to, then took the bicycle and went to Narcisa's house, where I found the windows half-closed as though in mourning for some misfortune, the dog was barking without much conviction but only to earn his keep and my brother-in-law without coming out yelled to me from inside to go to the hospital, there's only one hospital around here for some tens of kilometers and people who get sick all go there from every village and remain isolated without being able to give or receive news because visits are allowed only for one hour on Thursday and one on Sunday but in those two hours there's such a confusion of dialects around those crowded beds that you don't even succeed in communicating with your sick relative, and yet the patients always have the need to be talked to for example my grandfather when his leg was amputated the other patients had put the idea in his head that they had used his leg in the kitchen to make broth and so he no longer had any appetite and in a short time wasted away and died on a Tuesday and we learned about it on Thursday when he already should have been buried, this delay in informing people is a drawback that no one bothers about when it comes to bad news while for good news assuming they're good by giving a tip to the janitor and waiting outside in the street you can always know, at any hour of any day, if your child has been born and what sex it is, and this is such a great privilege that no one objects to the idea that having brought a child into the world you must also pay to find out if it's alive and what sex it is, it turned out to be a Thursday afternoon at the visiting hour and by getting in line I was actually able to enter the maternity ward of the hospital, here walking along a corridor stinking of urine like a latrine before getting to the women you pass a large room with many rows of little cages each with a newborn baby inside but some also with two because there are more babies than cages and of course the cages for a single baby are always reserved for the children of workers while the children of peasants have to be content to be in pairs separated by a glass looking each other in the face for days on end without saying a word like two lunatics, the room has two glass windows the peasants look at their double cages through one the workers look at their single cages through the other and that's what I did too mingling with the men and the odors of my race and vying amid the crowd of heads and armpits for an opening to see beyond the glass, but then something appeared that so held my attention that I forgot about trying to guess which was my sister's child: the glass of the window reflected the images of the peasants, projecting them as a group onto the group of babies' heads, and the ruddy and porcine expressions of the fathers were superimposed like perfect likenesses on the dull and malignant mugs of the children so that for a moment it seemed to me as though the lives of these babies had already been decided forever and conditioned by having those faces and therefore that destiny, as though their meaning all lay in growing up and coming on this side of the glass and aging in a hurry just to see replicas of themselves start all over from the beginning, and looking over there at the workers' babies less crowded and more rosy-cheeked with restless and delicate little fingers and their little eyes moving under their closed lids I became painfuly aware that before seeing the mask he has made for himself over so many thousands of years crumble crust by crust the peasant will have to scrape away at it for as many thousands and who knows if he'll ever succeed or if it's not better to give up and be content to exist as he is, I was also thinking that by now after so many centuries of injustice everybody is unjust including God Almighty and my father too thinks the way I do since he's never swallowed that story about a landowner who went out at daybreak to hire some workmen, and he sent them immediately, at sunrise, to cultivate his vineyard, promising them each one coin, and three hours later he sent more workmen, because it was a big vineyard, and three hours later he sent still more, and again after three hours still more, God knows how big that vineyard was, and in the evening he seated himself and they all stood around him waiting on their feet while he took his money out of his pocket, so many coins for the same number of workmen, and he paid each of them off with one coin: once when the priest in church, at early mass, while everybody was sleeping snoring wrapped up in their cloaks, said friend, I do not wrong you, for the money is mine and cannot I do as I like? my father got to his feet to say that this God Almighty was not made for us peasants who are treated like animals in this life and it would be only right if in the next life other people, city folks and workers, were to try being animals, turnabout's fair play, the priest completely shocked stamped his feet in rage and refusing to answer or to finish the explanation of the Gospels turned around and threw himself on the altar to continue the mass stretched out on the steps as though to make God Almighty believe they'd stabbed him and meanwhile the peasants woke up jostling one another disappointed and numb because they hadn't slept enough, for weeks the priest didn't come to see us because of my father and every morning my mother got up long before dawn for fear that God Almighty would unleash a storm on our heads and she'd light so many candles in front of the saints crowned with olive that from the smell of the wax you'd have thought you were in church, this business of my father wanting people to take turns being animals came into my mind right there in front of those cages separating the newborn babies into two categories, over there children with the faces of children over here children with the faces of little animals, and one of them was related to me, that one there with swollen purplish cheeks as though it had already been drunk in its mother's womb, or that one whose head twitches as though operated by a faulty mechanism, or this one with its oversized and disagreeable mouth as though it had been born only for the purpose of stuffing itself, and thinking it over again today it seems to me that my father's idea, which at the time I didn't completely understand, wasn't such a bad one after all and that without waiting for the next life it would be a good thing if even in this life our brutalized people were to wake up at a certain moment and say enough, let's switch places, now it's your turn, and get up the courage to enter the houses in the city, as in wartime when anything goes, and take a clean working girl or some beautiful city woman with a perfumed snatch and jump her right there laughing in her ear go ahead, have a little animal kid yourself, and I hope it's born with the tail of a jackass.

PART TWO

1. Failed magic

So when Panzetta, coming into our house without asking permission, appeared on the kitchen threshold, it was such a great honor that my mother was completely consoled and drying her hands on her apron didn't even ask him if he'd like to join us but immediately set in front of him the bowl with my food which Panzetta devoured noisily as a sign of reconciliation, and then explained to us that here was the chance to perform a lovely act of charity since my sister's departure had left a vacuum in our house that Providence was now offering us the opportunity to fill, for once again this year the villages in the Rovigo area had been flooded and families were being sheltered some here some there and he as our priest had already requested a few dozen children for our village and now he was going around trying to place them and to us he had purposely assigned a girl, named Patrizia, who would arrive next day on the bus with the others, and there was no need for us to go to any trouble except to pick her up in the village, the bus arrived all bedecked with streamers and little flags as though it were on a tourist excursion but no one was singing inside or waving handkerchiefs or smiling and when it stopped in the village square Julia Imbroja at the top of her lungs intoned hymns in which no one joined her and stood there warbling and craning her neck while the little boys and girls got off the bus handed down by a driver who read aloud the name written on the tag that each child wore attached to his or her collar by a little chain, when the driver said Patrizia I stood there gazing at her so as to make her acquaintance in secret and start off the encounter with a slight advantage, she was standing on the footboard of the bus her head lowered dressed in a red velvet skirt and a white jersey, she wore yellow knee stockings and black patent leather shoes with, instead of laces, a strip of red leather attached by a button, and she was the first and last woman I've ever seen wearing shoes fastened by means of buttons, the driver in the meantime had lost patience because it looked as though as far as Patrizia was concerned the hosts had changed their minds and hadn't shown up, so I stepped forward and put out my hand to take hers and she jumped down from the footboard and as she jumped her long black braid rippled on her shoulders, she had a round face, dark hair and very long lashes over blue eyes that shone too much as though from fever and with rings under them from suffering, like water lying unsullied in a pool traversed by carts, she was fourteen or fifteen years old but looked older especially because of the proper and superior way she behaved, we walked home holding hands and it was always she who asked questions because I was quite put off by her elegance and keeping my head lowered I looked at her buttoned shoes and my bare feet and could no longer tell whether she was still the one who had need of me or rather I who had need of her, in fact when we passed the cemetery and she said churchyard I immediately experienced a sort of revelation, it almost seemed to me that in her world the dead were more noble and respected and valuable and dignified than in ours, and all the way home no sooner did she stop looking at me than I in my turn peered at her out of the corner of my eye and from the way she moved her eyes and head and hands, and from the way she walked straight as a poplar with her head held high moving her legs without swinging the rest of her body and with the soles of her shoes barely skimming the grass I understood that she was delicate and born and raised in a different country, speaking different words in the midst of different things, in a house differently built, one that even had a floor of bricks or wood not like us peasants whose corns are always touching the bare earth and when someone has a cold the women put the heating pan full of coals next to his feet which doesn't do any good because the cold and dampness extinguish it in a few seconds so if you want to get any benefit out of it you'd really have to do like Rucolo who stuck his feet in the fire laughing I'm fine, when we arrived home Patrizia sat down solemnly in a corner and my mother hovered around her asking her if she needed anything, as soon as Patrizia asked for some bread and fortunately that month we had it I grabbed the sack from the bin and deposited it obligingly at her feet. From that moment on my memories get confused because I remember too many things about Patrizia which means practically everything she did in our house for the six months she

stayed there, starting with the first time she sat at the
table and said buon appetito and we sat there flabbergasted with our spoons in our hands not knowing what
to answer until my mother smiled at her and then
everyone smiled at her except my father who never
smiles, and ending with the day when she went away
with an oversized cake bigger than herself, but just
because those memories were deeply experienced
they've scorched my memory and I'm no longer able to
place them in their proper sequence, all I can say is that
from then on everything changed not only in our house
but in every family in the village, the city children
always wore shoes while we put them on only to go to
school or to church and took them off as soon as we got
out the door, our school is near the river to be exact near
the bridge leading to the church and consists of one big
room where all five classes are held, the pupils in the
first three are seated in such a way that their backs are
to the pupils of the last two because there are two
blackboards and two teachers, a man and a woman,
who ought to teach at the same time, but actually the
man who teaches the two upper classes is never there
because as soon as he comes in he distributes to each
pupil a little fable written on a piece of cardboard and
then goes off to the river to fish coming back at the end
of the morning to hear one or two summaries and since
he knows only two fables we can be sure that only those
pupils to whose lot they fall have any reason to read
them, while the others can do what they want, in good
weather when the fish are biting the teacher even waits

for us in the street with his wading boots up to his knees and the fishing rod on his shoulder and whistling softly he watches us arrive in twos and threes and enter the school helping us quicken our step with a smack on the rear then he marches off to the river to reappear toward noon throwing open the classroom door and holding up the catch of fish strung one after another by their gills on a wire so that the woman teacher can get a good look at it then he hangs it smelly and dripping at the blackboard, as a result of this fine habit the classroom stinks like a fish market and black white gray and striped cats are continually jumping up and down at the window sniffing with obvious interest and some even dare to dive into the classroom in our midst but then all the little boys throw themselves on it and in the uproar the boldest one succeeds in catching it by throwing his cloak over it and holds it up by the neck showing it around like a trophy to the woman teacher and the admiring little girls, the arrival of the city children put this system in jeopardy because they brought notebooks and exercises and from the very first day asked the teacher to correct them and so the teacher had to stay there among us and we made a circle around him although the matter irritated him so much that at a certain point not being able to stand the noise he sent out for some corn and stones and made the most rowdy pupils kneel on them, Patrizia and I would set out from home together and it made me proud that she could see I was carrying the log of wood for her too, the fact is that in the school there was a big stove and the pupils had the task of supplying

103

it with enough wood for a day each one bringing a log tied to his shoulders like a knapsack except the poorest children named in a special list nailed to the door who could warm themselves free of charge as for example Tojo who was so poor that not being able to buy blotting paper he brought a package of ashes with him every morning from home and he made his own ink by squeezing elderberries into a bowl. From the way she shook her head one could see immediately that Patrizia was very proud and indeed she always wanted to be the one to go to the village and buy the few things we needed at home, and in this my mother was happy to comply except that most of the time it was very hard for one to understand the language of the other and they had to have recourse to gestures or better still to examples and the result was that to send Patrizia to the store to buy four or five little things it was first necessary to borrow those little things somewhere and send the girl off with samples, the same difficulties emerged when Patrizia needed something and I in order to gratify her set out on it immediately but then went all over the house pronouncing the names of all the things that I saw in the hope that the sound would bring back to me something that rhymed with the name pronounced by Patrizia, half an hour would go by and Patrizia who had asked me for a *mela*, an apple, would get worried and come looking for me and would find me all alone and stupidly talking out loud before a big pile of *pumi* and giving me a curious glance she'd take an apple and nibbling on it curl up at my feet eyeing me a little suspiciously while I for my part so as not to admit total defeat continued my crazy rigmarole undaunted but more and more worried because the sound of *pumo* didn't rhyme with *mela* and to come to terms with Patrizia I saw no other solution but to learn wholesale the foreign language she spoke.

The number of children in the village had been almost doubled by the arrival of these alien city dwellers but it wasn't something that could be particularly noticed along the roads because these well-dressed and well-brought-up children were far more dignified than us peasants and each family treated its guest with every consideration, without making him or her do anything they didn't want to and putting all members of the household at their complete disposal so that they would declare their satisfaction whenever by chance the priest came around to see how things were going, thus my family too learned to flatter and pamper Patrizia in ways that no one had ever taught them and now for example my father, who had always devoured his meal in two minutes and gone out, now waited for Patrizia before starting to eat if she was washing her hands at the threshing floor, and in the final months when she said buon appetito there was my father on the verge of smiling at her like everyone else, and when he had to go upstairs to her room he announced himself before entering by making a loud noise and knocking on the door, and when it was the season for figs or grapes he went out early in the morning with a basket to pick the fruit before it was spoiled by bees awakened by the first

sunlight and for Patrizia he set aside the best pieces
leaving them in full view on the sideboard on a plate
that each of us was proud not to touch, and I competed
with him in serving her and showed her the clearest
pools of water and gathered the sweetest berries for her
and went fishing for her and carried all that wood for
her, to hell with Maria Panettiera whom I had once
mistakenly thought I liked, for her I'll never carry so
much as a stick because I want to serve you alone, I'll
take you where the quinces grow big, and with my long
claws I'll dig mushrooms for you, I'll show you where
the jay makes its nest, I'll show you how to snare a quick
slender weasel, I'll take you where the hazelnuts grow
in abundance, I'll catch blackbirds for you in the bushes,
will you come with me? we'll make a cricket go backwards out of its hole by poking it with a blade of grass,
I'll show you how with a pole to detach the nests the
oriole hangs like a basket, I'll teach you how to make
migratory birds come down from the clouds, how to
make fish rise to the surface of the water, I'll foretell for
you a moment beforehand the screech owl's cry, the
night bird's passage, the fall of raindrops, the heron's
flight, won't you stay with me? She listened to me
attentive but disenchanted, because by now I was her
dog and fire-stoker and keeper but everything I had to
offer diminished every day in value and in its attraction
for her so that standing there reduced to shreds like a
wizard whose spell has failed I came to realize that
actually I was only her pupil, and that my countryside
no longer had anything to teach to her city perhaps

indeed had everything to learn, and that everything we peasants know we should hurry up and forget if we want to become men for it may be just what we know that makes us resemble animals, you have only to look for example at a worker living on the city's outskirts he may not yet be completely a city dweller but nevertheless he's already different from us because he's finally freed himself from what we know and he goes to bed in the evening without hearing birds banging against his door and if in the morning he finds a puddle of water in the street he doesn't just stand there looking at his reflection in it but telephones the municipality to get them to come and drain it and he sleeps well at night only if during the day he's touched nothing but iron cement and plastic for if he's touched wood or trod on grass he tosses and turns in bed because of the return of his old anxieties, the fact that the heron steers clear of smoky cities and alights crookedly on our watery countryside means that we are as crooked and fluttering as it is, and when we detach the oriole's nest it goes and rebuilds it two trees away judging our action to be the momentary spite of a peevish fellow species, from that day on I started spying on Patrizia at every possible moment in order to steal from her the secret of her existence and teach it to myself and my family, but I was discouraged from the start because the whole thing seemed to me literally inexplicable, it wasn't that there was a secret in her behavior, only that she was born different and nothing could be done about it for example she didn't sit down at the table because she was hungry

but because it was a daily ritual one to be performed
nicely by raising your elbows in delicate movements and
barely opening your mouth and chewing a little at a time
and savoring in small sips and breaking your bread with
a couple of fingers of the right hand and a couple of the
left and in short behaving in accordance with well-
defined rules and movements that embarrassed us
because none of us had ever suspected that you could sit
down and eat for any other reason than hunger and our
father had set us the example by drinking his wine from
big dirty greasy aluminum pitchers emptying them in
one choking gulp that made his Adam's apple go all the
way up to his mouth and drop down into his stomach
like the plunger of a pump and when the soup wasn't
boiling hot he used to pour it directly into his gullet from
the plate without using the spoon that he now holds
unsteadily in his big black hairy hand, none of us had
thought that you could go to mass for any other reason
than to please the priest, and now here's Patrizia laying
out her dress on Saturday evening and polishing her
shoes and trimming her fingernails and fixing her hair in
ways my sister had never known how to do and
arranging her ribbons and all the rest and as she goes up
the stairs to go to bed she says goodnight to us her
enraptured audience and asks my mother to please
wake her up early and sure enough next morning she
comes down early half asleep in the dim light of the
acetylene lamp dressed in red with her shoes all buttoned and when she turns around she no longer has her
braid, it seems impossible, and yet there's no braid and

her head looks even smaller like a sparrow's with short hair like a boy, she couldn't have cut it last night, which means she must be able to take her braid off and put it on as she pleases going to sleep one way and waking up another unlike us who are always identical throughout the centuries and who keep repeating our ancestors even in our names because when in some household an old person dies and a child is born you can't ask what name shall we give him because otherwise the dead person will be offended and start playing tricks on you for it's as though you were denying him the right to set foot again on this earth, the sort of tricks the dead can play depends on the character of the deceased in life, with the dead members of the Brusacasotti family who are our village incendiaries it might happen that when the oil lamp gets overturned and your tablecloth is burned and you throw your jacket over it to put out the fire it doesn't get put out at all and instead your jacket gets burnt up too and you're left with nothing but your shirt, with the dead in the Spiandorelli family who in life have always been herdsmen which has given them the same melancholy smoking eyes as oxen it can happen that when you release your mildest most gentle and strongest ox from his chain so that he can go and drink from the trough he doesn't go and drink the way he's always done but stands in front of you and gives you a questioning look then you look back at him brushing a wisp of straw from his nostrils and ask him what's the matter? and at that very moment you realize that his eyes are not his bovine eyes but the human eyes of one of the Spiandorellis who bears you a grudge by now you're penned in between the ox and the feed crib with no way out and sure enough the ox stops chewing his cud and becomes serious then pensive then rambunctious and first he waves a horn back and forth under your nose so you'll get a good taste of it and even smell its odor and then quick as a flash he plants it in your gut, the only thing that can be done to avoid all these tricks is to satisfy the dead in every possible way and with your own family dead the shrewdest move and the one most consecrated by tradition is to detain them in this life by giving their names to the newborn and then verifying how the misfortunes of the living repeat in detail the misfortunes of the dead by saying every so often ah Jijeto has a sour look like poor Jijo or ah Jijeta is going blind like poor Jija and then a few years later ah Jijeto has liver trouble like poor Jijo or ah Jijeta is getting hunchbacked like poor Jija, and then a few years later ah Jijeto is getting married to a cross-eyed woman like poor Jijo or ah Jijeta is still waiting to get married like poor Jija and we can be sure that in the future our children will say ah Jijo died in a ditch like poor Jijo his father or ah Jija dropped dead like poor Jija her mother.

2. In search of the thermometer

That day when Patrizia whispered that she was shivering and had no appetite none of us was able to finish our meal, my father deeply concerned fixed her some mulled wine and he didn't try to estimate her temperature by passing his hand over her forehead as he would do with us making us feel as though we were being scraped by a cracked stone, but sent me to the priest to ask to borrow a regular thermometer, measuring a person's temperature is more complicated than measuring an ox's because the person gets hot while the ox gets cold and by feeling his ears starting at the tip you can follow precisely the progress of the cold that is the increase in fever when the cold arrives at the head if you look deep into the ox's eyes you see them change color and then it's time to send someone on the bicycle to call the veterinarian for it won't take long before the situation becomes serious when the fever will have invaded and occupied the animal's whole skull and he starts sneezing spraying big gobs of blue saliva all over the stall and shaking his head as if he had just swum across the river, if the veterinarian arrives immediately on a motorcycle sitting on the rear seat preparing the injection along the way and leaping into the stall picks out the sick ox in a flash and without wasting time sticks the needle in the rump then the ox with the help of Saint

Bovo may survive but if the veterinarian takes his time and stands there with lowered head speaking Italian and running through in his mind all the dictionaries he's studied then you can forget it because in the meantime the ox swells up and keels over with his four legs spread and his eyes and tongue sticking out on the straw and not even God Almighty could get him back on his feet now it's your wife who'll be your ox and she'll have to work twice as hard if she wants to get by and your daughter too had better stop playing the young lady always thinking up reasons to go to the village and show off, the priest didn't have the thermometer because ever since the city children had arrived all our fellow villagers had become more conscientious when it came to chills and fever and at their guest's first sign of indigestion they knocked themselves out pedaling along roads and culverts like racing champions to borrow the thermometer, the last ones to come and borrow it had been the Saonellas whom I barely knew by name but who according to the priest lived in the neighborhood of the Hump near where the Flying Fortress had crashed during the war, it really looked as though the Flying Fortress had wanted to die in our village because it had appeared on the horizon in the sky over Legnago keeping itself aloft with great difficulty and passing over had grazed the poplar groves of Santana and Oni and Be Osso and was finally seen to disappear at Marega and we all thought it had fallen there but a moment later we felt the houses tremble and a great column of smoke went rumbling up at the borders of our village and already we were all running full tilt each hoping to be the first to get there but the very first was One-Arm who in a single glance had already spotted the richest area for loot and drawing a line on the ground had taken possession of it and was sifting it inch by inch in search of screws and nails copper wire pipes sheet metal ball bearings springs which he was collecting and piling to one side where his stick stuck in the ground was like the signature of the owner, it looked as though the Flying Fortress had not fallen from the sky but sprung up out of the earth because the land was cracked and upturned as though from the sudden eruption of several volcanoes at the bottom of each of which there was now a piece of motor or a heap of smoking sheet metal, the water in the ditches had been heated and boiled while frogs hopped away so as not to explode or die poisoned by the oil and gasoline that floated with a sinister bluish or yellowish sheen that no one had ever seen before, and right in the middle ditch, the deepest, where the peasants kept going back and forth and so as not to lose any loot they sent word home that they would eat here for the day, were the armless torsos of three burned and charred men all in a row and it was no longer possible to tell whether they had been white or black.

The Saonellas lived right there by the Hump, where the banks of the river are very high with respect to the surrounding countryside and the ditches are always full of water and of frogs which produce such a hellish clamor with their croaking that two people can't even start a conversation with any hope of hearing each other, the Saonellas must be used to this and resigned since talking isn't the most important thing in this world anyway and you can live all the same working your ass off in the fields eating in the culverts shitting in the ditch because there's no cesspool where you squat on your heels knocking up your wife and dying with a groan, in short you can do everything, except anyone who arrives unprepared can get a headache and as a courtesy to him the Saonellas keep an empty barrel in the middle of the yard on which they pound with a stick, there was a time when as soon as the echo of the pounding passed in waves over the valley the frogs would shut up swarms of them diving into the water, but now the trick is old hat for them too and having increased in number they've become more daring and when they hear the boom they merely pause out of politeness and then resume their croaking so that to make conversation possible the Saonellas have to station a boy next to the barrel to beat the drum over and over like a volley of gunfire, between one volley and another you may succeed in exchanging a few words but you always go away with the feeling of not having explained yourself sufficiently although without the slightest temptation to turn back, worst of all there's no way of getting out quickly because the yard and all the surrounding area is a soft layer of mud mixed with the dung of chickens ducks geese and humans over which you can't ride a bicycle and can barely succeed in walking you sink up to your calves and with every step there's the danger that in lifting your foot you'll leave your shoe stuck in the quagmire and balancing yourself on one leg like a crane you must manage to retrieve your shoe before the mud closes over it, in dry periods when the level of the river falls a little the Saonellas throw blocks of bricks on the mud one jump apart and with the help of a pole they're able to hop from one island to another and arrive safe and sound on the river bank, that's the period when the Saonellas finally show up for mass with shoes and not boots, if it were possible with the use of large pumps to dry up all that foul-smelling bog all sorts of working tools and household utensils and mementos and other objects lost from one generation to the next would come to light, enough evidence to show the history of the Saonellas throughout the centuries, next to the door of the house they've dug a big hole that always fills up with water by itself and into which members of the family by common consent lower themselves to clean all the mud off their boots before going in the house for supper, so far as I could make out the Saonellas didn't have the thermometer either, a week before the Rapacinas had come to get it and they hadn't given it back, anyway the whole village knows the Rapacinas never give anything back and that when they ask to borrow something it's an open form of stealing, all the more since the Rapacina boy coming to get the thing was very surprised when they asked him who was sick at home and shrugging his shoulders answered impatiently nobody, obviously the attention of the Rapacina family council which meets once a week to decide on their ventures had been caught by the thermometer's sudden

increased circulation and therefore by its presumable
rise in market value, still this hitch didn't bother me
since to get home from the Hump I'd have to pass the
Rapacina house and so it didn't make my trip any
longer, as I slowly left the Hump and pedaled back up
out of that watery and greenish darkness toward a
normal light the great rumble of croaking frogs subsided
and my usual thoughts returned, above all of Patrizia
lying in my sister's bed looking at the wall sweating and
silently awaiting my return, at this thought I was
ashamed to have forgotten about her for a while and
consoled myself with the excuse that in all that uproar a
person could even forget who he was otherwise why
would the Saonellas ever go on living there with rats
under their beds, now here was the Rapacina house
buried under the poplars and vineyards so badly built
that it's even impossible to figure out the correct layout
of the place with all its additions of little rooms and
closets constructed of lumber and branches and mud
and sun-dried bricks with low and narrow doors
through which you'd have to enter by crawling on all
fours like a cat, these are the storerooms and hiding
places for the thefts systematically committed by the
Rapacinas in neighboring villages and sometimes in
ours too, everyone knows the Rapacinas are thieves but
no one dares denounce them to the police and indeed if
one of our villagers gets a feeling that something is up
and gets out of bed and going out to look around his
fields at night hears a sound as of someone harvesting
his grapes free of charge, it would be a good idea for him

to creep closer while hiding in a ditch to see who it is and if it turns out to be a Rapacina then he'd better pretend he's seen nothing and go home because that time the Lindis thought they could just jump out and claim their rights first of all they got beaten up there in the field and then a year later all of a sudden their grain piled on the threshing floor catches fire and goes up in smoke while the poor Lindis not knowing what else to do dance around it screaming and rolling on the ground, the Rapacina house is completely dark because the windows are small and inside there's no illumination other than the fire which is always lit, it's not yet evening but already the Rapacinas are all there engrossed in eating sitting around the fireplace and not at the table which anyway isn't there and holding their plates on their knees without speaking they chew with loud relish and as soon as I appear on the doorstep and ask to borrow the thermometer the kids look me up and down with glittering eyes licking their chops and the head of the family stares at me ceasing to move his jaws and agitate the mouthful of food that now motionlessly swells his cheek, then putting his lips back down to his plate like an ox in the manger he chases the scattered crumbs all the way to the edges with his snout then licks the plate with his tongue and hands it to his wife who goes out and puts away in the shadows a clean plate shiny as a mirror ready for the next meal with no need to be washed, now the man spreads his legs out on both sides of the fireplace as though to roast his balls at the flames and though he has nothing in his mouth he goes on grinding his teeth giving them a useless workout and I realize that poor Patrizia will get no response from him so I might as well go I turn around but now that I can see better my eyes having become accustomed to the dim light I discover an old man with red eyes and lips pinched with bile seated like a child on a big armchair with no straw bottom to its wooden seat and with a big hole in the middle obviously for his bodily needs, underneath between the legs of the chair and aligned with the hole is a huge terracotta chamber pot held up by strings and more than big enough for a whole week at the end of which it might even get emptied, the old man has been staring at me for some time with his sharp little eyes and he wags his shoulders constipated as he is as though at that very moment he'd at last succeeded in doing something but that's not the reason rather it's the effort at thought that his archaic brain structures are making and indeed when his agitation is over the crisis dissolves in a sudden upward motion of his chin as though it had been released by a spring and he says to me hey! take it, so I turn around and though unable to see her face take the glass thermometer, gleaming in the flicker of the fire, from the hands of the old woman who had already been there ready to hand it to me and I go away still without having been able to tell whether there were seven persons or seventeen in that family, now that I have the thermometer with me I hold it up with one hand like a trophy while I pedal home to arrive before nightfall which in this season comes on the world all of a sudden so that if from an open road exposed to the sky you enter a tunnel of trees where you see less you think it's because of the shadows but then you come out and you see still less because now it's evening and those sharp sounds you hear among the trees are the birds slipping under the cover of leaves taking advantage of the last flicker of light by which they can still recognize their sleeping quarters, a few dribbles of light leak from the windows of my house but you don't smell the usual odor of carbide meaning that tonight my father is using the oil lamp which is cleaner and more hygienic and burns without leaving any residue in the air and besides doesn't consume much oil its one drawback is that if it's overturned the oil spills and the flames spread first on the table where we eat and then in sparks along the floor, the peasants have their houses blessed often for the specific purpose of exorcizing these dangers and when the priest comes to sprinkle his benediction in the rooms walking through them one by one all members of the family gather in advance to receive the holy water and no longer be unclean, I once happened to upset the lamp which besides for the reason that I'm the best behaved member of the family and don't move very much because I have things to think about always gets put next to my plate and from there might just as well have been put on it with the food, on that occasion everybody stared at me obviously pondering and trying to remember whether or not I'd been present at the last blessing, I hadn't been present, next morning my mother decided to take me to school herself and when we arrived I understood why you see before taking me to school she took me to the church which is right there on the other side of the river and there she spoke in a low voice to the priest who kept nodding his head and answered loudly yes my dear yes my dear, I was standing outside the door watching the scene and I saw Panzetta from behind with his arms outspread in the form of a cross raising and lowering his head and when he lowered it he looked like a decapitated bust, then the priest walked toward me and standing upright at the top of the steps blessed me repeatedly with great sprinkles of water that gave me gooseflesh since I was wearing only my undershirt like almost all my school companions on summer days when skylarks are everywhere, aside from the danger involved the oil lamp still works better than the acetylene and the reason is that in every family the acetylene lamp is as battered and dented as an old artillery shell because the children play with it by unscrewing the lower part which contains the water and carbide from the upper part which contains the outlet for the flame and the screw to regulate the escape of gas, and they run off with the lower part into the open countryside and there make the carbide react with the water on a brick covering it all with the upside-down acetylene half on which they pile stones so that the explosion can occur only when the accumulated gas really builds up, with this system of blasts the Maio kids call those of the Mill or the Sand Pits, the kids of the Vigri district call those of the Lowlands or the Seven Chimneys, the kids of the Crossing call those of the Headland or the Cemetery,

the kids from the Big Ditch call those from the Levee the
Rich Fields the Woods and the Peak, and sometimes all
of them combine in squads and with great machine-gun
bursts try to rouse and summon the kids from the
boundaries of our village namely those from the Desert
the Swamp the Hump and the Dog Man, but from those
parts no sound has ever come back and the only answer
to our calls is the clumsy flight of some big wild bird, in
the evening before dark the children scatter and rush
home across the fields to put back the acetylenes which
by now are so crooked and dented that they no longer
stand up straight and have to be propped with a little
polenta or a piece of bread which by tacit and unani-
mous agreement is taken out of the child's ration.

When I go into Patrizia's room I see that my father
and mother are there with her, the room is well lighted
by the oil lamp set in a corner on the floor and I take
advantage of it to display the thermometer immediately
so that Patrizia can know that I was the one to go and
get it, but since no one asks me where I got it it's clear
to me that everyone will think I found it at the priest's
and therefore could have come back much sooner
instead of lingering to watch the fishermen on the boat
anchored in the middle of the river or the carts passing
over the bridge transporting peat with the carters asleep
and the mules ambling by themselves along the familiar
road, now my father is looking at the thermometer and
my mother holds up the lamp so that he can see that
strip of color through the glass which you see and don't
see, now you can see it, not much fever it's nothing

Patrizia, if tomorrow her temperature hasn't gone down then I'm to take the bicycle and go and call the doctor, I'm proud of the new assignment and glad that Patrizia has heard in fact I'd like her to know that neither the priest nor the Saonella family had the thermometer and decide to tell my father about it right away before he goes out of the room he stops lost in thought and asks me where'd you get it I say at the Rapacinas then he turns and repeats at the Rapacinas? I confirm that it was at the Rapacinas and immediately he admonishes me take it back to them later meaning after Patrizia has recovered, of course I'll take it back to them in fact we'll go together by bicycle Patrizia and I so she can see how far I had to pedal, now we're alone and I ask her if she'd like me to write to her parents to tell them she has a fever, she says she can write herself if I'll mail the postcard, which means she doesn't yet know that here we give our letters to the postman who comes by every two or three days always more or less at the same hour and that means in our parts around noon, all you do is leave a child in the road with the letter in his hand complete with stamp or if you don't have a stamp with the equivalent in cash and sure enough the postman stops and checks everything as well as trying to decipher the address and himself writing the sender's address on the back of the envelope, if something is wrong the postman goes in the house and makes them spell out the name or village of the addressee and with his pen he writes it again in capital letters crossing out the wrong name and writing above it INCORRECT and as a reward for his work all you have to give him is a glass of wine, that's why you can sometimes see a kid waiting at the gate on the road with a letter and the money for a stamp in one hand and a glass of wine in the other so that the postman doesn't even have to go to the trouble of getting off his bicycle but can do the whole thing while standing comfortably with one foot on the pedal the other on the ground his elbows on the handlebars and his backside in the wind, I tell Patrizia that here you just have to wait for the postman it's not even necessary to go someplace to mail the letter and that the postman should even be coming by tomorrow because he hasn't been here for two days and he has the professional obligation not to leave the village without mail for three days in a row, Patrizia is reassured and says she wants to write the postcard and that in her notebook there on the chair are some cards with the stamps already stuck on them, I help her to sit up in bed lifting her by holding her under the armpits and squeezing her to me with such increasing joy that I feel I'll never leave her again and will always hold her this way and I'll keep my face buried in her hair which has a special smell of civilization that I'll never stop breathing in order to transform myself, while she gets ready to write sitting up in bed and holding the postcard on her knees I bend over to her level which means that I find myself practically kneeling beside her on the floor and I watch her as she carefully writes in beautiful letters Dear papa she pauses a moment then adds and mamma I have a fever come as you said you would Patrizia, tomorrow morning just for you I'll wait for the postman myself even if it should rain in fact I'd be glad if it rains hard to show you that I can be as obedient as a scarecrow which wherever you put it there it stays, and I won't prepare any glass of wine because your letter is correct and the postman who reads it looking for mistakes will go off through the dust thirsty and put to shame.

PART THREE

1. A foreign language

Next day who should come into our yard with the first dawn breezes but the village herald I mean Julia Imbroja as usual bubbling over with high spirits and announcing to my mother that the Catholic Workers' Association had organized for next Sunday a reunion of the visiting children with their parents, therefore Patrizia's father would also be arriving at ten o'clock and we would have to go and pick him up in the village square because that's where the bus would stop and where it would leave from in the evening, la Imbroja was even more jubilant than usual and it was hard to see why, was it from the knowledge that this time people would have to recognize that she did things properly or did it come from a more developed civic awareness namely pride in the fact that some thirty city people would be arriving to visit or rather see our village since there was nothing to visit and in short would implicitly recognize our usefulness and entrust themselves to us, thinking back on it today I incline to the second explanation because once again I see before me la Imbroja with her fleshless and almost hairless skull the rough skin smoothed like paper and pasted over the jaws and teeth and neck bones laughing expansively and winking almost as though to signify that such heartfelt jubilation ought also to be ours, at that hour I was already awake at the window thinking of Patrizia with a great sense of happiness and confused mortification and for some reason I was looking over the fields at the fires burning here and there to thaw the frost that was ruining the crops, from those smoldering fires emerged a dense and choking smoke that rolled sluggishly an inch above the ground and traveling across the fields melted the thin coating of ice on the delicate leaves of the plants thereby saving their lives, you ought to know that if the night is to bring frost you can already smell it in the evening by breathing with your nose up in the air and concentrating your attention on the throat to see if it gets dry or moist or by taking a dog outside and watching to see how it dilates its nostrils in breathing or driving wasps out of their hole with a stick and seeing if they fly in a taut and orderly formation or straggle laboriously, even bats are useful because with their keen sensitivity they always fly crookedly to right and left up and down noting the slightest presence of tiny gnats and swooping on them with open mouths gulping them directly into their stomachs and discharging them immediately out behind but when the evening turns out to be damp and muggy then even the bats are fooled amid the dense spirals of water vapor descending in columns among the trees in the yards and you hear them throwing themselves about in vain and squeaking with empty mouths and sometimes in their disorientation banging against the walls of the house and with difficulty resuming their search in a world that is no longer familiar, on these occasions the peasant who has planted beans or is raising tobacco or other crops with susceptible foliage eats his meal with his mind elsewhere his hat pulled down over his eyes and hardly speaks to his wife and after supper when people usually put out the lamp and go to bed you can be pretty certain that this evening he has something to say and sure enough he decides that tonight he won't sleep but instead go and light fires in the culverts just like last year at this time and now he's assigning sentry duty every two hours and the midnight shift namely the hours of greatest danger he reserves for himself or for his male children who know how to mix wet earth with dry and piss on the fire so that the smoke is more abundant and effective, in families where there are no male children there's always however a daughter who just missed being born a boy and knows how to behave just like a boy namely to conduct business deals with feed and livestock dealers buy pigs by choosing at a glance the very one that will grow the fattest drive three pairs of oxen by herself in plowing and so she's the one who'll go into the fields on the most precarious shift and every so often if she doesn't find damp and burning straw or rotten leaves she'll straddle the fire with her legs and piss a few drops on it like a tomboy and what's more she may even have fuzz on her upper lip, the news brought by la Imbroja made it superfluous to send the postcard written by Patrizia to her father, so there was nothing to do but give her card back to her immediately that is before going to school, actually while I took the card and on tiptoe crossed the loft separating our rooms and opened the door of the room

where Patrizia slept I saw clearly that this reason was a
mere pretext and that all I wanted was to see her
sleeping and so then closing the door ever so slowly
behind me I lingered a moment to hear her breathing
and guess whether she was awake or asleep, but the
rumble of my heartbeat deafened my ears making it
impossible for me to distinguish such faint sounds and
I could only see indistinctly by the stale and dreary light
that filtered from the cracks in the widely spaced
windows, Patrizia was sleeping quietly on the bed her
feet close together her legs parallel and the shape of
her little body delicately apparent under the sheets
and her head was turned to the right with her arms bent
at the elbows and her hands half open one on each side
of her head, you could see at the level of the chest the
delightful rhythm of her breathing because a thin wrin-
kle in the sheet kept appearing and disappearing and for
a long moment I looked at her before going close and
lightly touching her face and I felt as though I had never
seen her before, on her face in fact on both sides of her
nose were a number of little freckles and her eyelids for
the moment looked closed and yet always on the verge
of opening and already I was imagining her bewildered
and questioning look but I persisted just the same
because now I was only imagining and no longer
thinking, or rather I was no longer even forming images
but was immersed in a single indefinite state of mind
that was half devotion to her and half self-abasement, to
look at her and remain in the innermost area of her
influence made me a better person and I would have

liked to become as much like her as possible I would
have liked to become her and without my being aware
of it there emerged from my throat a few words in
Italian for example *mele,* and saying *mele* I thought of her
as of myself and of myself as of something else and I
said *sapone* and I said *siepe* and the more I contemplated
her and repeated her Italian words the more I felt inside
me that every moment was fleeting and that I would
never again be able to remember it and that all these
obscure sensations would be lost forever under vulgar
words, and never again recovered except in the form of
pain for their loss, who in this village would ever be able
to imitate her civilized pronunciation and already from
that moment on I felt I was suffering a lot and I was
enjoying my suffering which refined me and made me
less unworthy and I consigned myself to her open and
questioning gaze for what I was, without sin and
without time, repeating *mele* which rhymes with *miele*
with the vague sensation of being born only now but
therefore of having at least begun in the presence of
someone who was already perfect, listening to my
enraptured soul unite and return from me to the world,
from the center to the circle, from the point to infinity,
walking within the new world of correct words like one
who has been pardoned for his errors and freed and
accepted and therefore feels precious to himself since he
had been as though dead but is almost resuscitated, he
has been as though lost but after all has been found
again, and you have come all the way here from the city
of properly christened things to find me I mean to let me

seek and find myself with your words which you scatter without seeming to like someone walking and leaving his footprints, and now that I've found myself that is found my place I'll never go away from here again and I'll stay and watch over you till dawn and till sunset I need you and your words and your pronunciation and your way of being and slowly going out I watch her for a long time and being careful not to make noise I close the door, as soon as the door was closed I went back to being what I was before that is with my usual words because it didn't make sense to speak Italian with all the people who were not Patrizias and as I looked at myself moving about there in the loft I saw all the things around me present themselves again one by one with their old stupid names and with a shabby and guilty look the way a dusty gang of mercenaries reassembles and closes ranks around its leader after being defeated, then I went down to the kitchen and sadly ate polenta with milk and went to school, in school ever since Patrizia had come I had been reading more carefully the little fables that the teacher distributed to us and when in my fable the words I had heard from Patrizia did not occur then I'd borrow from some schoolmate the one that had been assigned to him and when I hit on the perfect phrases that coincided so well with what happens in cities as for example *un paio d'ali per volare*, a pair of wings for flying, then I repeated them aloud and the reality I had always had before my eyes corrected and improved me because the word *volare* is something noble and courteous and well mannered and ceremonious and straightward while *solare*, the way we say it, is crooked and crude and unmannerly, this must happen because in the city they see *volo* as straight and long and high while we see *solo* as something quivering and fantastic that springs out from under your feet and is already gone, and *sapone*, soap, is something that as soon as you touch it so perfumes your hand and fingernails and face that you seem to walk in a nice-smelling cloud while *saon* is the black oily dirty kind with which my father washes his hands when they're greasy with naphtha and fertilizer with the result that his hands are just as greasy as before and all those who wash their hands after him should they then sniff them will find them stinking of naphtha and fertilizer for the rest of the day, these aren't different words that indicate the same thing but different things correctly indicated by different words so that in order to change words and pronunciation you have to change environment, it's ridiculous to put our *scugliero* in your mouth almost as though it were a choice spoon like the one Patrizia holds in her hand with such perfection, all these differences are summed up in the very figure of Patrizia who even in her name proclaims herself as something other than our Assuntas Concettas and Carmelas and the Doroteas who are the most numerous because Dorotea is the saint of our village, and the teacher became aware of this sudden passion of mine for reading from the time when he had asked me to summarize the fable that had been assigned me as it turned out one of the few that he knew and I had summarized it for him with emotion and a precision of words and inflection that left him flabbergasted, from then on he had also ventured to ask me about the fables that he didn't know so as to find out more or less what they were about since now that there were these city children he had to stay there in the classroom and in some way pass the time while trying not to make a fool of himself for among the new arrivals there were also some older ones who were more advanced in their studies and came to our school only so as not to be idle and not unlearn everything and one of these was Patrizia who had never been flunked and in her city attended eighth grade, also now at home I was not only reading all the books I had a total of three including the catechism but also Patrizia's books and her back-issue magazines and besides I had had her listen to my summaries she who after all was the only real teacher I had had in my life, for the entire week that her fever lasted I would come to visit her bringing the decoctions of herbs prepared by my mother and I helped her to drink them by lifting her up to a sitting position in the bed and while she leaned her head against me I squeezed her softly and gave her a report on the morning at school and I read to her whatever she wanted while waiting for her to get sleepy so that I could contemplate her secretly in total sincerity without having to assume a feigned attitude, during those days my mother went to the fields to look for the most effective medicinal herbs which only she knew, and so Patrizia kept getting visibly better so that in the end she didn't suddenly get sleepy any more and for me the opportunities to contemplate her and transform myself occurred less and less often until Sunday came and Patrizia feeling recovered wanted to get up and wait for her father.

2. Intuition of the city

What fascinated me most when Patrizia's father arrived was the way they went and threw their arms around each other as though they wanted to demonstrate their love not to themselves but to the whole world, and immediately there came to my mind the reactions shown by my brother and sister and me when our father unexpectedly came home from the war a year before it ended, he arrived on a bicycle without tires because if it had had tires the Germans would have confiscated it from him but being without tires he had trouble keeping his balance because the wheels kept wobbling from side to side making the bicycle swerve suddenly in ways that required a lot of maneuvering with the handlebars, and with his whole body getting jolted every time a wheel struck a rut or went over a stone, while the stones dislodged by the metal rim shot out to right and left like bullets, and still a lone German who was making an early retreat on foot with a big knapsack on his back and his head bending so far forward to lick the dust that between Italy and Germany assuming he got there he wouldn't have seen anything but his own shoes against the background of various roads, the minute he heard the grinding of the wheels straightened up like a bow freed from its string and planting himself with legs spread in the middle of the

road almost in front of our gateway barked ALT ALT
ALT he grabbed the bicycle as though it belonged to him
by divine right and jumping on it and arching his back
gave an energetic push to the pedals that sent him
straight and quick as lightning into the water in the
ditch where he re-emerged sputtering and spent with
the knapsack on his back and a leaf on his head and on
the leaf a frog to resume his trek to the infinite on foot,
meanwhile my father had already come in the yard and
gone from there to the closest fields where he paused
looking around with the eye of an expert touching the
shoots and leaves of the vines and resuming his trust in
the earth, then extending his gaze farther he walked
toward the fruit trees and by scratching the blisters of
sickness on the rotten bark with his black fingernail he
guessed which parasite worm it was and muttered
through his teeth red spider red spider while we children followed him in silence at a respectful distance not
even daring to hope that he had noticed us but still glad
to be able to look at him, and finally with slow steps our
father turned back to the house where my mother was
already waiting for him observing him through the
windowpanes and at the door of the kitchen she said to
him take that thing off and she took the pack off his back
and then asked with concern have you eaten and when
my father answered in a low voice oh sure nothing and
sat down lost in thought his head between his hands,
my mother immediately went to take the pot from the
pig rinsed it a little because we're clean people and hung
it from the chain in the fireplace mixing water and flour

to make polenta and then approaching the window through which we children with our noses pressed against the glass were peering secretly at our father she motioned to us to go away and leave him in peace, so we went gloomily in Indian file to the yard between the house and the barn and sitting there we waited for my older brother to say something since it was up to him to interpret the new situation and lay out a program and give us instructions, but our brother in whom two souls were combined one practical and explosive and one lyrical and thoughtful was obviously at that moment in the grip of this second soul and therefore sat there with knitted brows his bowed head resting on his hands which he'd taken out of his torn pockets and raised his face only when a great wave of tolling came floating on the wings of the wind and it was then that he gave his higher interpretation which rang out like an order directed at the universe ring the bells because he's come back, that had been our reunion after four years and now Patrizia and her father are hugging each other and rejoicing because they haven't seen each other for a few weeks, her father wears glasses and every so often he adjusts them on the bridge of his nose with a spontaneous little gesture of his right hand, on the breast pocket of his jacket three letters are stitched in yellow gold OMP which I read Omp and don't understand neither does my father and after they've greeted each other with a clap on the back the first thing my father asks him is what does Omp mean and the other one who was waiting for just this question answers officine

meccaniche padovane, Paduan Machine Shops, and
gives an ugly laugh looking at my father in triumph, so
he works in a machine shop and now that he has an
employer he looks down on my father who is like a stray
dog without a collar at which my brother already starts
grinding his jaws in anger, now the city father lifts up
his daughter making her skirts flutter and greets her
with his news hi little Paduan, what a little Paduan,
when you come away from here we're going to live in
Padua, right in Padua, we're working in Padua now I at
the machine shop in the San Paolo quarter, your mother
at a lawyer's in Santa Trinità, and your brother'll have a
job in a store in Via Sacra Famiglia, my mind is dazzled
at hearing this string of holy names and immediately the
endless images of the city that I'd absorbed helter-
skelter from Patrizia's books and illustrated magazines,
read and re-read for days on end drooling with antici-
pation and learned by heart, arise and mingle in my
head, and now here was the city just as I'd always
imagined it Santa Trinità must be the heart of paradise
where the gentleman doctors and professors are, around
it there's the Sacra Famiglia where the merchants live
with their stores windows shops barbers bars, close by
Sant'Antonio with its miraculous piazzas, proceeding
outward from there the successive rings of the outskirts
that by embracing the center share its light and heat and
movement, Jesus Mary and Joseph save my soul, San-
pietro Sanpaolo Santalucia Santanna Santagnese Sant-
elia and who knows if there may not also be our
Santadorotea with places reserved for emigrants from

our village, depending on the importance and authority
that one acquires little by little he'll obtain the right to
change neighborhoods and slowly approach the center
with all its mirrors windows doormen benches on the
sidewalk where anyone who's tired can sit down and
rest his legs, extra braids for women, ice cream thrown
away that still hasn't been licked by dogs and you can
pick it up with your fingers by the tip of the cone,
banana skins with a bit of the pulp still untasted there
inside at the end where the flies can't get to it, doves
that come and eat out of your hand and peck your
fingernails as though they were grains of rice, music in
the bars for those who pay but maybe a smart person
can fool everybody by stopping in the street pretending
to be deep in thought and so get to listen to it for
nothing, illustrated magazines tossed into trash cans
that are waist-high so you can pause beside them for a
minute or two and then put your hand in the can and
pull out a magazine as if it were yours that you'd thrown
away but had now changed your mind and wanted to
read all over again looking in particular at the pictures,
women wearing tight trousers and walking arm-in-arm
and as soon as they've gone by you can gaze at them all
you want while they call to their boy friends on the
other side of the square going yoo-hoo just like that
yoo-hoo so that someone'll rush up to them excitedly
and say here I am, old men with white hair and short
pants and from the way they look at you from the pages
of Patrizia's magazines you realize they're rich and that
you'd better be careful if there's something they need to

gratify them, girls who walk off down the street with gold chains on their hips and from the way they make them jingle with every step you understand that they're moaning release me for God's sake release me, steps going up and down on which there are always a lot of girls because from below they're on display and by slowing their pace they seem to say look at me to humanity, beggars who lie flat in the dark corners beside latrines with a plate in their hand and as they watch the world go by they seem to say even if you don't give us anything we're happy to be here just the same, dogs their fur clipped their backsides sprayed with soap their eyes cleaned with cotton that when they have to go they do it somewhere aside in an old shoe under a flue or in some other kind of stew and not like us where the crudest boys do it by climbing the trees along the road and hiding among the leafy branches so as deliberately to hit by surprise anyone passing underneath on a bicycle who anyway unless he's an outsider has by now acquired the healthy habit of wearing a wide-brimmed hat pulled down in front, learning Patrizia's magazines by heart I had come to know the city thoroughly and those who lived in it and some nights I had even dreamed of visiting it rediscovering there all the human figures encountered in the illustrations and recognizing them one by one, the girl in the yellow overcoat adorned with big blue flowers embroidered in relief and a neck scarf who first appears on the pages from the front but with her face turned in profile and the scarf over her mouth as though modestly hiding her laughter and then from the back as she walks away with her hands in her pockets her elbows bent and her head tilted slightly downward as though displeased she was waiting one evening on the steps of a bridge that overlooked a small square swarming with sounds and people and as I pass by daydreaming I see her and going up the first steps I gaze at her while the breeze stirs a lock of her hair raises her scarf and hides a smile and she starts down toward me and passes alongside me with her face turned directly toward me so that for a moment we look into each other's eyes and in the next moment I see her going away her head bowed her elbows bent and I'm wounded to the quick by the certainty that a little while ago she was looking at me but didn't see me, the girl with the white silk dress with red squares on it and in each square a blue dot I had seen her from a distance at a street crossing and at that moment she was struck by a slight breeze and her whole dress fluttered spreading its countless folds and as it fluttered it looked as though inside there couldn't be a body, waking up next morning I rushed into Patrizia's room to check if such a thing were possible and in fact looking at the photograph I saw that it was practically as though the tiny little body weren't there, you couldn't see anything but a head large but light with a lot of hair and two big eyes like two green spots with the outlines vaguely indicated, so many straight deep folds descended from the neck that they seemed to bypass the body all the way to the knee and the sleeves kept puffing out and descending little by little toward the long thin fingers with their pointed nails, it really made you want to squeeze her to find out if she was inside that dress or not and just how far she'd shrunk, and the girl who over her white dress, with pleated skirt and blouse embroidered with seasonal motifs bunches of grapes for instance, wears a very long and slightly flaring jacket in red and white wool with a pattern of stripes and circles and a white half-belt attached with a button on each side just a little above the waist, with a huge violet kerchief around her slender neck, she went by with her left hand dangling freely at her hip and the right on the gilt buckle of her military belt walking with a quick step and not giving a damn about all the people sitting in the square who had stopped reading their newspapers or were putting down their drinks or adjusting their eyeglasses or giving a whistle while turning to look at her, well even from Patrizia's magazine that girl looks straight ahead intent on her own business and however I folded the page or shifted my position to meet her gaze she always came out looking proudly absorbed in some other direction, with all those people in the squares and on the streets and in the churches and in the trams you're never alone in the city and by following along behind a couple telling each other their experiences you can find out immediately what's happened to them and by mingling this way with the crowd in the markets and stores and where the trams stop you can hear the stories of all the others and it's as though you were living not only your own life but many other lives as well and it seemed to me that if I were able to live in the city I'd

143

sleep every night with one ear cocked until the sounds of the crowd finally faded and every morning I'd rush to the window to see if the people were still there and in a few days I would have discovered the places where you see more people and in rush hours I'd be there to enjoy with my eyes my ears and my nose the whole flood of human figures who come and go admiring and paying each other compliments so close together as to hurt each other and not leaving so much as an inch of space to solitude, and it seemed to me that in the city you could do without the calendar since by looking out the window at the people and observing for a moment the dresses of the women the colors the fabrics the style you could know right away we're at the beginning of April or May we're in the middle of September or October we're at the end of August, because the city is a completely new world that moves and grows by its own specific rules and only by living there for a long time but always scrutinizing it day and night is it possible to discover its mechanisms one by one and learn how they work and take your own place in it and call yourself a citizen.

I was thinking all this sitting in the yard when my mother came to call me to dinner, and going in the kitchen I saw that everybody was already sitting at the table and that Patrizia's father had taken my father's seat without even asking, he made broad gestures while he ate and kept talking in a loud voice about career and salaries and vacations and turning every so often toward the open window he took deep breaths saying such air as though the air were good while the truth is that there was such a strong smell of hay that at a certain point my mother taking this outsider's words in the opposite sense got up to shut the window while my brother grinding his jaws followed her with his eyes, as he took big spoonfuls of soup the visitor passed the spoon under his nose as though he wanted first to breathe the broth and then swallow it and in short savor it twice, and after the soup while my mother was changing his and Patrizia's plates he got up and going to the window looked again out around the yard repeating over and over you lucky people so that my father and brother stared at each other more and more bewildered and suspicious not knowing what there was to feel lucky about but already my brother was beginning to think his leg was being pulled and his jaws trembled in irritation and I was looking at Patrizia fearing that our families wouldn't part in perfect harmony, fortunately my mother at a certain point reminded everyone that in an hour there was to be the great procession organized to celebrate the reunion of the children from the Delta with their parents and so while the visitor asked about the religious rituals of our village my brother hurriedly bolted the last of his food and gulped down one after another the glasses of wine he was entitled to and casting the last angry look at the beautiful golden shining letters OMP on the visitor's breast pocket he went away red-faced and furious a half hour early as always on these occasions because he was one of the Bearers the strongest fellows in the village whose job during processions is to organize themselves in teams of four and carry on their shoulders the saints of our church, Saint Anthony, Saint Dorotea, and the Holy Family, this last being a group of tall statues standing upright on a base so broad that during the procession it fills the whole street and no one can pass without dismounting from his bicycle and walking on the grassy edge of the ditches naturally with his head bared as a sign of respect for the saints of our village, that time that Majotto from Marega pretending to be deep in thought came pushing his old bicycle held together with wire his head down and without lifting his hat at a certain point a violent blow came from the procession that knocked his hat on the other side of the ditch and nobody ever knew who did it nor for that matter could Majotto have had any wish to find out standing there in the middle of that long line of people who were doubled up laughing uproariously in his face and even on the lips of the priest there was a certain little smile of satisfaction, that was the first and last time that Majotto crossed paths with our processions because from then on if he really had to go through our village on Sunday he kept his eyes open and if he saw the cortege he rushed into the first yard he could find or behind a hedge or off through the culverts so as not to be seen, the worst time was when some guys from Marega, the people in Marega are really our enemies but some day we'll clobber them for good, insisted on passing in a rattling old wreck of a car sounding the horn from a distance so that the procession would move aside, on that occasion the priest sent a member of the Confraternity of Candlebearers running, although he couldn't run very well with his white soutane down to the ground and his little red cape and in his hand the candle which is two meters high, to order the car to turn around and stop blocking the way, while the procession was advancing very slowly with great effort and sweat on the part of the Bearers those guys from Marega got out of their car and started arguing with him heatedly even daring to raise their voices in proclaiming their rights which at that moment was nothing less than sacrilege and they didn't shut up even in the presence of the priest who was so angry that he couldn't even speak but kept stammering and sputtering saliva while his eyes smoldered, at the rear above the surging mass of infuriated people the statues of the Holy Family could be seen tottering fearfully as the Bearers passed the word among themselves to set the saints down quietly and go and beat the hell out of those bastards and chase them across the fields as fast as they can run, we'll see if they have the guts to come back and get their car, in fact it was two days before they came to get it first sending an emissary to our priest to settle the quarrel and insisting that the priest come to the door of the church so that the villagers could see that he'd peacefully given a kind of verbal safe-conduct.

The procession that day was like all the others, proceeding across the bridge and all around the Mill district which is the center of our village and for the occasion it was decorated with tablecloths and lights at the windows and flowers in tin cans on both sides of the

completely empty streets, at the end of an alleyway
Berto Oco could be seen watching the cortege with
staring eyes and his body contracted in paralyzed confusion until his tension was released as soon as someone
ran up to him to drag him out of the way and without
letting himself be caught he disappeared panting around
the first corner, Panzetta chanted in a loud voice words
more Latin than usual and you could feel he was
anxious to make a good impression on the city folk
perhaps in the hope that they'd report it to the bishop,
Panzetta is always sure of himself but he stands in great
awe of the bishop and in fact when on the occasion of
the passage of the Pilgrim Our Lady the bishop came to
our church and kneeling with a hammer in his hand
tapped the floor tiles and the marble of the altars and
columns of the balustrade to check their state of preser-
vation our Panzetta with his fellow priests from the
nearby villages followed him step by step steadily
swallowing his saliva in the fear that there might be a
loose tile and when the bishop stood up and laying the
hammer down on a chair clasped his hands together
Panzetta behind him heaved a great sigh of relief and
immediately imitated him, when later the bishop seated
in the armchair in the middle under a large pharaonic
umbrella flanked on both sides by priests during the
sung mass leaned over toward Panzetta to say something to him emotion suddenly clogged the ears of our
priest who didn't understand a word and looked around
in confusion sweating and swallowing his saliva while
the bishop with a broad gesture of his right hand much

admired by all the faithful began to smooth his long beard, it was too bad that because of his awe and emotion and also a touch of deafness Panzetta cut such a poor figure that day because the whole village was magnificently organized to celebrate the Pilgrim Our Lady life-size dressed in white gold and blue with her arms spread slightly open and her head, tilted delicately to one side, adorned with hundreds of little gold chains offered by the girls of the villages through which the statue passed, in our village we had even collected a great quantity of kerosene to fill a number of tin cans which were lined up on the iron parapets of the bridge and lighted one after another as the cortege passed at night creating for everyone the religious impression of Hell, just at that point the friar preacher standing at the center of the long line of people and who with his high voice dominated the sacred chants started speaking of hellfire and then you could see some people quicken their step and detach themselves from the crowd to run secretly to the confessor who always stood waiting and I thinking I had conceived the surest method of saving myself from Hell by scratching the Madonna's feet and swallowing the plaster dust when I was able to approach the statue without being seen realized that the feet had already been scraped many times by others with the ends of their fingernails, you could see long particularly persistent streaks where the plaster was the softest, I stretched out a hand as though to help the Bearers in their mulelike effort and with my thumbnail scratched a little dust and then raising my hand absentmindedly to my forehead I sucked the thumb feeling the dry plaster dust soaking up saliva on my tongue, at that very moment I raised my eyes and saw the Madonna turn jerkily in my direction and stare at me in an indescribable way and my tongue already dry from the plaster went completely parched and my legs were as though tied together and my brain numb while the whole line of the procession went by leaving me there on the flaming bridge and only after half an hour was I able to move and go home where for penitence I went to bed with rocks in my underpants which next morning my mother when she remade the bed found in the sheets and threw out the window without asking questions, whatever may happen to me in the rest of my life that will always be one of the things planted most deeply in my tortured memory.

To form the procession in orderly fashion the members of the Confraternity of Candlebearers first take their places with their large candles always lighted and protected against the wind by a glass bell which is removed only on re-entering the church, there are fourteen Candlebearers placed in two rows seven on each side both while walking in the street and when the procession is over they re-enter the church where they arrange themselves standing along the balustrade, it may sometimes happen that not all fourteen are present and then Panzetta as soon as the mass has begun turns around from the steps of the altar and looks at the crowd of the faithful and picks out some suitable men and calling them by name gives a nod of his head toward the sacristy, they go in and find the bell ringer with soutanes in his hand ready to dress them, after the Confraternity of Candlebearers come the girls of the Company of the Lily each wearing a white veil and with a lily in her right hand and then the women with black veils and then the men and in the middle of them the priest with the book in his hand surrounded by the altar boys one of whom holds above his head the pharaonic umbrella and behind the priest the Bearers divided into three groups first those with the Holy Family then those with Saint Anthony and last those with Saint Dorotea, finally bringing up the rear the children, when the triduums are held they don't carry the statues but they do carry a portrait of Saint Bovo who protects the oxen from hoof-and-mouth disease and then the procession stops for a long time with the portrait conspicuously displayed at the doors of the stables struck by the disease and here while Panzetta speaks his potent and incomprehensible words it is up to a member of the family being punished by heaven if it cares about its interests to hold the saint and guide the chorus of litanies taking for a moment the place of Julia Imbroja who out of respect for hoof-and-mouth disease willingly gives it up while standing there ready to guffaw and shake her head the minute the singer out of an exaggerated wish to sound good resoundingly hits the wrong note, on reaching the borders with the village of Marega where there's a stone beside the road with Marega inscribed on it the procession doesn't do an about-face but turns to the side and starts back with the leaders still

151

in front and each of the two lines turns toward its own outer side thus winding its way back between the edge of the ditch and the elbows of those faithful who are still going forward to reach the boundary stone, which means there's a moment when each person sees all the other members of the multitude pass alongside him and you can even exchange a greeting or a word or two if it's really necessary, this happens naturally between the men since the women and the girls with lilies always have their heads bowed in mortification and it's also this public mortification that perpetuates over the centuries the feeling that women always have a great sin to atone for making them in the final analysis deserving of contemptuous treatment by men, I was not far from the men and at the point where my line turned back on itself I saw Patrizia's father looking very pleased and nodding yes yes with his head as though everything were going well and meeting with his approval and following the line of his gaze I saw that it ended with the perplexity of my father, on the bridge Patrizia's father had stopped for a moment to look this way and that with an admiring air as though to say what a nice place while raising his hands to the sky, so that by now not only my father but all the people who were watching and feeling the pompous amazement of this outsider were looking at him with the suspicion that he was pulling their leg, it also ended up being an embarrassment to us who were giving hospitality to his daughter so when the procession was over we weren't sorry to be told that the bus was waiting in the square in front of the tavern ready to depart immediately with all its passengers, and now here comes our city worker holding Patrizia's hand and adjusting his eyeglasses on the bridge of his nose and as he sets his foot to board the bus he hugs his daughter once more bye-bye little Paduan lifting her up from the ground so that her skirts flutter then he says goodbye to us too with a broad wave of his hand and a condescending smile and before he disappears we see him smooth his jacket by passing his hand over the pocket with the glittering letters OMP.

3. *The marvelous vision*

Patrizia stayed with us for another couple of months in which time I had the chance to read and learn by heart the new illustrated magazines her father had brought her, especially during the last month when school was over and having been promoted with good marks I had nothing to do, so I spent hours and hours in silence without even answering when my mother called me hiding in the shadows of the barn or hayloft with a bundle of Patrizia's magazines on my knees hurriedly leafing through them and committing to memory all the illustrations of human figures and neighborhoods and lighted streets and then I'd close my eyes and mystically absorbed see all those images once again but connecting them in a proper and orderly fashion against a single background and placing the odd and less lively persons with some defect in their gestures or clothes on the outskirts while slowly amassing in the vortex of the center the more perfect human figures whose eyes were accustomed to the bright light of day and night and the women whose look overcomes you and who even from the pages of magazines force you to lower your eyes and make you ashamed of yourself, this would even happen to me for whole days during those idle weeks and at nightfall I would get up and brush away the spiders that without my noticing had got up my sleeves and down

my back and up my pants and I'd go looking for Patrizia
in the yard or in the fields and talk to her for the sole
purpose of drawing inspiration from her and the
strength for a new vision that might come to me that
same night or the next day, the news of my promotion
had been conveyed by the teacher directly to my father
and accompanied by the suggestion to have me study
land surveying because, at this point the teacher instead
of explaining what he meant with words had raised the
index finger of his right hand to his right temple and
performed a drilling motion which is a gesture that
among us can mean that someone is intelligent or,
depending on the context, that he's crazy, and where
the context isn't sufficiently clear it means that one
interpretation is as good as the other, from that moment
on people in the village getting ahead of themselves
started calling me ditch-jumper which is the local ver-
sion of land surveyor, now on the basis of Patrizia's new
magazines and the names of the neighborhoods and
streets in Padua that I'd heard from her father's lips I
decided I was capable of constructing for myself a plan
of the City by tracing a number of concentric circles like
a kind of target in a shooting gallery and on it I began
conceiving the stages of my immigration and marking
them in red, taking it for granted that I would never be
able to arrive at the true center of Santa Trinità except by
the clandestine path of intuition and then only for a
moment or two, but by hoping that from the farthest
outskirts I would be able to make some small approach
about every five years I managed to die along the ring

named for the Apostles Peter and Paul, though before dying I would certainly from there be able to see mirrored in the sky every evening the great illumination of the center much better than what at the time I'd been able to see from our house, in the hazy nights, of the great and rarefied meteors of light hanging in the sky over Legnago or Montagnana when they're holding a feast in those places and my jubilant mother calls me to come upstairs and from the windows of the loft we stand in silence and watch for a good part of the night and when the wind turns in our direction it even seems to us that it brings to our ears a breath of music and then we look into each other's faces enraptured without however saying did you hear so as not to interrupt the spell while below in the kitchen my father and brother have finished their meal and not giving a damn about it all they go proudly to bed extinguishing the lights with a violent puff which is to be understood as a puff of scorn directed at us, in fact my father and brother don't really need light and this I had understood ever since the evening when my father didn't succeed in making the acetylene lamp work though by putting it close to his ear he could hear the carbide hissing inside and therefore producing gas but this gas couldn't be lighted with the match because it sputtered and died, after only ten or so attempts while my mother still went so far as to insist saying try again you don't want to leave us in the dark my father and brother went out to the thresh- ing floor with the lamp and there by moonlight they set it upright on the block and by hitting it hard with a

mallet they made it explode and triumphantly brought
the hot metal plate into the house setting it in the center
of the table like a trophy and that evening we ate in
silence by the dim light from the coals in the fireplace,
the City must necessarily be organized in such a way
that everyone feels the attraction toward the center and
thinks of it continually and gravitates around it and
from it derives his happiness, but much as he may see it
only from a distance this won't make him unhappy
because he knows that the center exists and that it's
there and from it light and life and music and everything
he is come to him because after all it's enough for him to
have escaped the countryside to have emerged as by a
miracle from the quicksands that bring the most awful
death there is because there you can't even say I'm
dying for the minute you open your mouth it gets filled
with mud and silence so that in the end it's as though he
were already dead while he's still struggling and out-
wardly gives signs of life as all those I know in my
village seem to do and all those I don't know and will
never know buried in the oblivion of green darkness
with their animal sufferings and their ancestral appeals
and their bodily needs hunger thirst sex nothing else
ever happens because everything is as motionless
as the water in the sinkhole where putrified rats and
swollen cats with bared teeth float, you have to get out
of the sinkhole and into the flow of the river with the
religious certainty that even the current that hugs the
banks though it moves more slowly is still moving
toward the sea and in this direction lies your destiny

and the achievement of your destiny and therefore your happiness, for the whole last month that Patrizia stayed in our midst before going out of my life forever I tried to draw from her the best possible suggestions for the purpose of later being able to move by my own accord and not lose the impulse and find myself forever stranded like a car without gasoline in the middle of the desert and as soon as Patrizia had finished reading a magazine and put it down on a chair I would immediately take possession of it and study it pondering deeply on the thoughts and concepts included between one comma and the next and transcribing on a sheet of paper all the addresses I was able to find in it no matter what individual or company or institute or organization or association or news item they referred to and then I learned them by heart so that I could write them down again in case I lost the sheet of paper and I arranged them not in alphabetical order which wouldn't have been any use to me but in the order of importance of the saint for whom the street was named and in this way I was preparing my penetration strategy in accordance with a plan whose weak point was precisely its first element, indeed I was unable to put together an address in which the street appeared as dedicated to Saint Dorotea and I didn't know whether this resulted from the fact that entrance was denied to emigrants from our village since no one had ever gone away or perhaps rather from the fact that on that street there was no individual or company or institute or organization or association or news item of any particular importance,

this latter thesis finally ended by persuading me as soon
as I tried to imagine my fellow villagers transported to
the city and saw them standing wrapped in their cloaks
and repentant under a traffic light not knowing whether
to walk or not and in some way wanting secretly to
return home at once, then still to be considered was the
idea that the Via Santa Dorotea was a street of temporary
residents from which sooner or later you departed to
make room for some new arrival who is also your
brother, it was logical therefore that in such a street
nothing lasting would occur of which Patrizia's magazines would make any mention, all the more since those
magazines all came from the center as it was easy to
deduce from the illustrations and though it's understandable that anyone on the outskirts is interested in
the center it's by no means understandable for anyone
in the center to be concerned with the outskirts, the
mechanism by which an immigrant was propelled from
one ring of the city to another wasn't clear to me maybe
there was a Messenger honest as an angel who came to
announce to you that you'd earned the right to approach
the center, anyway this was something I'd find out in
due course, the important thing for now was to figure
approximately how many years were to be spent between one stage and the next, perhaps in the Via Santa
Dorotea less than five years would be enough let's say
three here we can mark 3 in red on my map over the
farthest and widest and slowest ring the one that least
feels the influence of the center of Santa Trinità, then
from each successive ring I shoot forward every five

years but perhaps this period can be shortened by some task of special merit and certainly as soon as I know what it is I'll do my utmost to carry it out thoroughly and devotedly, so let's say four years for each circle and we can calmly mark 4 and 4 and 4 and 4 over the various circles that enclose the untouchable boundaries of Santa Trinità, and at this point in my spirit I was carried away by emotion and had a marvelous vision, Santa Trinità is no longer a circle because It doesn't enclose but is self-sufficient and it's up to the others to enclose It and It is arranged in the form of a triangle Father Son and Holy Spirit, I believe in one God, Almighty Father, creator of heaven and earth, of all things visible and invisible; I believe in Lord Jesus Christ, born of the Father before all the centuries: God from God, Light from Light, born, not created, of the same substance as the Father. He suffered under Pontius Pilate, died and was buried, on the third day he rose, according to the Scriptures, and ascended to heaven, where he sits on the right hand of the Father: He will come in glory to judge the living and the dead, and His kingdom will have no end. I believe in the Holy Spirit who spoke through the Prophets; I believe in one Church, holy, Catholic, Apostolic, and Roman; I believe in the remission of sins, in the resurrection of the flesh and in eternal life. Amen, every corner gives on a street that branches off in a straight line toward the infinity of the outskirts and that straight line intersects the various concentric circles and from it they systematically derive their proper portion of good, it follows therefore that

along the same circle you don't have the same constant
and undifferentiated quantity of good because little by
little as you approach the radius coming in a straight line
from Santa Trinità the good increases and therefore the
circles are not in themselves motionless for periods of
five years but uninterruptedly at every moment there is
a continual shifting in them from receding points to
points exposed to this influence and this teeming and
disciplined swarm is proof of their life and of their
happiness and of their understanding of good and
perhaps if up there an account is also being kept of
everything I've suffered, even should I never arrive in
the Santa Trinità quarter, it could still befall me to die at
the corner of no matter which ring, there where it
intersects the straight radius and the blessed eye fixed at
the Center.

Author's note

I wish to point out to the reader that any references to real events, persons, and places are to be taken as the fruit of imagination; but I wish also to point out that the social background of the novel is true to the smallest detail, and that everything here written is essentially real.

The literary references are too obvious to require comment. It should suffice to mention a series of testimonies relating to beatification collected in *Conoscenza religiosa*, no. 1 (pp. 49 ff.), Jacopo Passavanti (pp. 28 ff.), the *Storia di Michele minorita* (p. 43), and the scene in which the monster Caliban encounters the human figure (pp. 106 ff.).

There is no printer's error on page 77.

Almost all the names of saints herein mentioned can be found on the street map of Padua.

Paul Claudel · *A Hundred Movements for a Fan*

Louis Couperus · *The Hidden Force*

René Crevel · *Babylon*

Stig Dagerman · *A Burnt Child*

Stig Dagerman · *The Games of Night*

Stig Dagerman · *German Autumn*

Grazia Deledda · *After the Divorce*

Grazia Deledda · *Cosima*

Grazia Deledda · *Elias Portolu*

Heimito von Doderer · *The Demons*

Marcellus Emants · *A Posthumous Confession*

Per Olov Enquist · *The March of the Musicians*

Péter Esterházy · *Helping Verbs of the Heart*

Ennio Flaiano · *A Time to Kill*

Peter Paul Fuchs (ed.) · *The Music Theatre of Walter Felsenstein*

Carlo Emilio Gadda · *That Awful Mess on Via Merulana*

Andrea Giovene · *Sansevero*

Remy de Gourmont · *The Natural Philosophy of Love*

Julien Green · *Avarice House*

Julien Green · *Each Man in His Darkness*

Julien Green · *Midnight*

Julien Green · *Moira*